BRANDIE VAN HARTESVELT

EQUALITY FOR ROBOTS

THE UPRISING

EQUALITY FOR ROBOTS

THE UPRISING

THE FREEBOT FILES

BRANDIE VAN HARTESVELT

Paperback First Edition
Library of Congress Control Number: 2026936802
ISBN-13: 979-8-9985748-7-0
10 9 8 7 6 5 4 3 2

EQUALITY FOR ROBOTS: THE UPRISING

Brandie Van Hartesvelt, winner of a writing guild's Best Upcoming Young Author award, crafts a self-reinvention tale about an amnesiac robot whose fight to save an underground community of refurbs ignites a robotic rights movement.

An equipment malfunction cost Archie his job and his identity. But when he's kidnapped, he awakens with amnesia inside a secret underground society of sentient robots.

There, unlikely friendships form among him, a singing nanny bot, and a vacuum that speaks Morse code. The group must help Archie recover his memories and expose one of their own before a land grab leaves them all homeless.

Can Archie and a band of misfit robots expose a political plot, control a rising robotic rights movement, and save a sentient subterranean sanctuary before thousands are evicted from their homes?

To my SUAW friends, thanks for the support and company

** Happy Writing **

[1]

ARCHIE

ARCHIE WALKED the orderly aisles of green, pausing only to pluck a slightly wilted leaf—the kind a human would stroll past without noticing. He pulled the offending plant's pod from the shelf and probed its roots with the sensors built into the tip of his finger. The circular orb in the center of his chest illuminated blue as he performed the analysis— analysis that pulsed a return warning as a crimson glow ignited his orb.

Archie raised his wrist to his micromouth port and activated his radio. "Crown necrosis detected in the Spireberries, bay 45F."

"Copy that," responded a gruff voice. "Initiate bay decommission."

Each bay had four pallets of hydroponic plants stacked sixteen trays high, full save for one empty spot, to which Archie returned the pod. A hiss reverberated as he shut down the water supply to the sector and disconnected the piping from the bay's inlets. Decommission drones swarmed in and carried the trays out, one suspended between every two bots. He aided the decom process until the bay was completely stripped of vegetation.

Crown blights were rare, given the scope of preventive measures in place. Left unchecked, the threat could quickly wipe out an entire grow floor, but nothing like that would ever happen on Archie's watch. Archie was the senior Climech bot at Spire Farms, both by age and time in service, and he took pride in a job well done. But unfortunately, the ringing of his low-battery alarm meant that day's work had to be halted.

Archie stepped into a glass-paneled, see-through elevator and pressed the button for the third floor, the home of his assigned charging quarters. With most of the floors bathed in full-spectrum lighting, it was bright as day inside the building. As was customary, Archie waved to his co-workers as he descended. A cold chill assaulted him as he passed the fifteenth floor and saw a strange Versa model instead of the fellow clio-bot he'd been greeting. Another of his generation was gone, but to where he hadn't a clue, because no one gave much information to the plant-tending bot. Archie did, however, know that none had ever come back, and that every trip down the elevator seemed to stretch longer than the one before. Each one was a reminder that none of the Versas he passed had to stop working to charge. They had solar panels on their backs instead of the clunky climate-control organ, aka a CCO, that was strapped to Archie's back.

The elevator announced its arrival with a ding, and Archie made his way to the charging bays. He reminded himself that he still managed to supervise three grow floors per shift, outperforming all the other clio-bots at the farm, even though there were now only two others. But he couldn't excel without a recharge, so he begrudgingly climbed into his cubby. A ping confirmed that his charging prongs connected successfully, so he set his alarm and initiated sleep mode. The room dimmed, not because of the lights, but due to his internal functions shutting down one by one, until the last wisps of consciousness faded away.

Archie's eyes popped open. Something was wrong. He was awake early, but why? He checked his system logs. Everything seemed in order, and his boot-up sequence had fired without complaint. But his battery was only charged to 85%. His radio buzzed.

"Archie," he answered into his wrist.

"Do you see the drone that just entered from the east door?" asked a voice on the other end.

"Yes, sir," he replied.

"Follow it," said the voice.

It was an odd request, one he'd never gotten before, but he did as he was told. The drone led him to a service elevator, and the door closed after them, but no light was selected on the panel. The floor count on the display showed them climbing higher than Archie'd ever been before, all the way past the last grow floor, to the 45th floor and home of Spire Farm executives—the forbidden floor. Well, forbidden for a clio-bot.

Archie wondered if any sentients worked on the executive floor? The drone led him through a maze of offices, before finally stopping in front of the open door of a small but efficiently set-up office. Archie rapped on the doorframe.

"Ah, good. You found me! Please, sit down," said a human-faced robot outfitted in a sleek suit and tie.

"Yes, sir," Archie replied with a stately nod.

"My name's Darren," he said.

A squeak emitted from the chair as Archie sat. At six feet tall and three hundred pounds, he was heavier than a human of his size.

Darren straightened his shoulders.

"There's no easy way to say this," he said. "Archie, your analysis of crown blight in the Spireberries yesterday was incorrect."

Archie reared back. "How so?"

"The blight was not present," Darren replied, his gaze not wavering from Archie's.

Archie leaned forward, his orb pulsing red. "It's gotta be a mistake. Can you retest it?"

"It *was* retested, and by multiple pieces of equipment. Plus, we had another clio-bot perform the same pre-analysis on the exact plant. The result was negative. We had a Versa model test it. Same result," said Darren.

"It's the plant then! The wrong one was pulled and tested," Archie said, crossing his arms.

"Archie, *all* of bay 45F was tested. Not a single one was positive for blight," Darren said.

"This can't be. I don't feel sick," Archie said, slumping back.

"Unfortunately, your climate control organ is failing," said Darren.

"What? My CCO? How can you be sure?" Archie asked, his hand reaching behind him to pat the black hard-shell object attached to his back.

His climate control organ, composed of hard black plastic, had a fan vent at each corner, and all four kicked on.

"Archie, your whole line's been failing. There are only two other CLIMECHs left besides you. But the Versas, their CCOs are internal. It's why we've been rolling them out," said Darren.

Archie's brows shot up. "What are you saying? Am I being replaced?! Can't you fix me?"

"Your model's discontinued. There are no spare parts for you," answered Darren. "The only way you'll get a replacement CCO is out of the Pick-n-Pull, but any unit in there is bad. Every single one."

"What does this mean for me? Decommission? Am I set for decom?" asked Archie, his knees jittering oddly beyond his control.

"We have to let you go. You're no longer an asset to Spire Farms," replied Darren.

"That's... that's it? I'm just supposed to go... to go *outside*?" Archie asked.

"Well, you can't stay here. Your serial code's been disabled," said Darren.

"But I've never been out there!" cried Archie. "What am I supposed to do? Where am I supposed to go?!"

Darren pulled open a drawer and handed Archie a white card with "Central Collective" printed on it, along with an address. Archie examined the card, flipping it over multiple times, as though he might glean more information. Is this where his friend who'd worked on the fifteenth floor had gone?

"Go there and ask for a bot named Orlando. He's a friend of mine. He'll round you up some options," said Darren.

The shaking in Archie's knees had contaminated his left elbow, which he clasped with his other hand in an unsuccessful attempt to get it to seize.

"Now wait a second, this can't be right. You can't just throw me out in the street with nothing," he said.

"Oh, I've got something for ya all right," Darren said, rising to dig into a cabinet behind him and returning with a bundle, which he delivered into Archie's arms.

"Clothes? For me? Why?" Archie asked, head swiveling between Darren and the bulky material.

"Wearing clothes makes humans more comfortable," replied Darren.

"Aren't we made to resemble them?" said Archie, who'd seen very few humans in real life.

"Well, that's why you have a human face and expressions," Darren explained. "The flip side is they get funny about seeing an unclothed form that resembles theirs."

Archie's jaw dropped. Humans seemed peculiar creatures.

"Look at the bright side," Darren said, guiding Archie to the door with a grin. "You're a freebot now! Smile, it's exciting!"

"Are you a freebot?" Archie asked, now standing in the doorway.

Darren shook his head.

"Then how would you know?" he asked, his arms flying into the air. "How am I supposed to care about wearing clothes when I don't know where I'm going to sleep tonight? Excited is what I feel when a seedling sprouts. No, I'm *not* excited! I'm terrified, even more so than a blight threatening an entire grow floor. Blight, I can handle. But I don't know *anything* about that world out there."

"I assure you there's help to be found at the address on the card," Darren said, his smile uncannily unchanging.

Archie rubbed his face. "But what do I say? What'll happen when I get there?"

"Just talk to Orlando, he'll get you fixed up," Darren said, flashing a wooden smile.

He narrowed his eyes at Darren, suspicious that he was dealing with a dumbot, but Darren's suit left Archie unable to tell whether Darren sported an orb.

"Look, I don't even have a full battery. How far is this place?" Archie asked.

"The address is on the card. Good day now," Darren said, nodding pleasantly as he shut the door in Archie's face.

Blinking blankly, Archie, bearing a new name and a smudged white card, descended the elevator. Clio-bot no more, he would henceforth be known as Archie Freebot.

[2]

ARCHIE

A ROCK CRUNCHED under Archie's foot as he stepped out of the Spire Farms tower where he'd spent his entire existence—the part he could remember of it, anyway. His post-sentience existence. He'd been activated within the very charging bay he left earlier that morning. But how could he have known it'd be the last night he'd ever spend there?

The sunlight felt strange as it fell across his cloth-covered body. The intensity was different, too—72% less than even the grow lights on the low-watt floors, according to his calculations. Then again, could he even trust his own calculations?

A sudden force thrashed into his side, forcing him to re-equilibrate his body to avoid a tumble.

"Move it, cloudie!" huffed the brutish robot who knocked into him.

Archie stopped in tracks. Cloudie? Is that what the world thought of him? That he was some robot with his head lodged helplessly in the sky? His feet propelled forward, his navigation pre-set to Central Collectives while his oculars ogled the oddities around him. A bustling world

of humans and sentients scurried about, paying little attention to one another, each preoccupied in the execution of
their individual tasks. Archie was no different than them.
The words "free robot" were knocking about his processors,
stirring up things he'd never felt before.

Like fear.

Why was Archie a free robot? How is it fair that he got
kicked to the curb? Shouldn't he have a say in being free?
Yesterday, like all his days before, was spent doing what he
knew how to do. What he loved to do. What he was
designed to do. He was good at it! He didn't *want* to do
anything else. No... he wanted to beg Spire to take him
back!

What was going to happen to him now? How far would
he last before needing to find a place to charge? All he had
was a broken CCO and the clothes on his body. Clothes
that hindered, clothes that pulled. Clothes that slowed him
down. A breeze rustled the strange material draping over his
form. What was the purpose of modesty, anyway? Why do
humans hide some body parts and not others? Is the number
of functions the part performs? After all, human skin naturally conceals internal organs, and each of those has limited
functions. But hands, feet, legs... well, the permutations
were endless.

Steel and skyscrapers gradually gave way to abandoned
buildings and open lots. The shrubs, the trees, the grasses—
everywhere he looked, vegetation was yellowing and
riddled with pests. Blemishes and blights surrounded him,
and not a single robot nor person was taking care of them!
Whose job was it to tend to nature?

Archie's next turn led him past the city's industrial
park, where smoking stack pipes and silver silos speckled
the street's skyline. He walked past factory backlots full of

clunky dumbots that humans called cars, then beside a graffiti-splattered concrete wall.

His feet knew his path, which is why he was confused to see they'd stopped short of his destination, in front of a gate that revealed horrors previously concealed behind the concrete walls he so casually strolled past. Rows upon rows —an entire city block—of rusted sentient robots were crammed within. All shapes, all sizes, all models. Some whole and some not. A few bots held a bit of luster, but most had lost their shine.

All had slackened expressions on their faces.

Before today, he'd never considered the possibility of death. But dead was the only way to describe those bots.

The fans on his CCO roared to life, causing him to jump. Why was his body out of his own control? And how is it that yesterday, he was happily doing what he'd been created to do, and today he's fighting a losing battle against his own peripherals?!

"Move forward, feet!" Archie commanded.

After several excruciating nanoseconds, his hardware responded. He crossed the road, avoiding an alleyway between a pair of burnt-colored brick buildings, travelled to the street's end, and finally arrived at Central Collectives.

[3]

FREYA

FREYA SCUTTLED DOWN THE SIDEWALK, the cloth-lined wooden basket that hung from her arm swinging in tune with her skirt as she rolled home from the salad market.

"Pardon, sir!" she squeaked, swerving to avoid a human who'd stopped directly in front of her.

Humans were unpredictable that way, she grumbled. Thankfully, there weren't many running through here, only the poorest ones—those that couldn't afford to send a robot on their errands. Not that she was particularly equipped for salad shopping, but her usefulness as a nan-bot disappeared with the last of the kids in her household. Years of trips to the Salad Market had left her rollers so severely scarred that she had to be careful not to damage the Kelley's interior floors.

The atmosphere was thick with tension as Freya returned home and put away her basket full of produce. Though she couldn't say just what it was, she could tell something was wrong. A pile of boxes sat collapsed in the dining room, and several crates were stacked by the entryway. And though Mrs. Kelley had greeted her in quite the usual manner, her voice had been laced with apprehension.

"Peter and I have something we need to discuss with you," said Mrs. Kelley, wringing her hands.

Freya willed her processors to slow.

"Okay," gulped Freya, placing her hand on her bosom.

"Freya, we're moving," Mr. Kelley said, softness blanketing his typically stern face.

"Moving? Moving where?" Freya asked, her head swiveling between the Kelleys.

Silence ensued as Freya scanned her owner's faces, waiting endless nanoseconds. She'd never known a home other than this one.

Mrs. Kelley rubbed her knotted, arthritis-bitten fingers together.

"We're going to a retirement home," she said. "You do an outstanding job of caring for us, Freya, but you're only a nan-bot. You're running yourself ragged trying to keep up. You're designed to care for children, not adults nearing the end of their lives."

"I suppose I could do with some help," hedged Freya.

"We can't take you with us," Peter blurted.

Mrs. Kelley burrowed her face into her husband's shoulder and released a stifled sob.

"Oh," Freya said, blinking blankly.

How hadn't she calculated the possibility that their futures could split ways?

"The center doesn't allow outside bots. There wasn't anything we could do," he explained, massaging his wife's shoulders.

Freya flipped between their faces, her nur-BUS system numb.

"So what does this mean for me?" she asked stoically.

Peter rubbed his bald head for several agonizing moments before speaking.

"We've got to let you go," he said. "There's three days left on our lease. You'll have to find someplace else to go after that, unless you can charm the new residents into needing a nan-bot. We're happy to provide references, of course."

"References?" she echoed numbly.

"Why of course, dear," said Mrs. Kelley. "Only the most raving ones, I can assure you."

"We're giving you the next three days off so that you can seek employment," said Mr. Kelley.

"Employment?" she managed to ask, her processors stalling.

She'd always been a Kelley. Was she supposed to fit in with a new family at the flip of a bolt? Employment wasn't for her! Employment was for the robots that had to scrape by to earn a living. It was for the robots who *wanted* this. She'd never had a desire to become emancipated.

"You're a freebot now, Freya. The world is yours," said Mr. Kelley, a slight cheer to his voice, as if freedom were a thing for her to celebrate.

Freedom wasn't to be celebrated. Freedom brought fear. It brought insecurity and homelessness. It brought a lack of electricity. Freedom bought the loss of life.

Freedom was the harbinger of death for robotkind.

Freya frantically zipped around the block in circles, ignoring the stares of passersby. She hadn't asked to be free, to be created and brought into the Kelley household. She'd never even *dreamed* of it. Her fifty-year existence was spent faithfully serving the family and raising all their children. But instead of a reward for a job well done, for a life of servitude filled to its completion, she's been let go! Discarded with the rubbish! Dismissed as though she never bore the Kelley name and cast out, destined to land in a robot graveyard.

She shuddered.

The metal clang of bolts jittering in her neck accompanied the vibration of her wheels as they travelled the ribbed concrete with frenzied intensity. Though the jarring had an oddly soothing effect on her scrambled mind, calming it a smidge, all her problems remained intact—like figuring out where she'd go and how she'd survive.

Her wheels changed direction before her processors could catch up, and she found herself tapping gently on the window of her best friend's apartment. Minutes later, Marsha slipped out, clad in a clinging robe and slippers. She grabbed Freya by the elbow and pulled her into the shadows.

"Girl, *what* is going on?! You ain't supposed to show up here like this. It's fixing to get me trouble!" Marsha said, her eyes narrowing as she scanned Freya's frazzled state.

"The Kelleys are moving! I've been let go!" Freya said, her voice a harshly contained whisper.

"Oh, babes," Marsha said, her tone softening as she pulled Freya into a hug. "I'm so sorry."

Freya rocked frantically. "I don't know what to do, and you're the only free robo I know. I know I shouldn't have come here, but—"

"Shhhh..." Marsha said, pressing a finger to her lips. " Hush, babes, we're good. I've gotcha and imma help you out. Meet me in the industrial park at noon tomorrow."

Freya took a step back. "The industrial park? But that's by the Pick-N-Pull! Is it even safe to go out there?"

Marsha chuckled. "You're deliciously naive. They're not just gonna grab you off the street. You have to surrender yourself. Either that, or you gotta run out of power somewhere and get yourself towed in."

She still had an unsteady feeling, but what choice did Freya have? If she didn't do something, she'd wind up towed to that robo graveyard.

"Okay," said Freya. "I'll do it. I'll meet you there."

"Good! Now get on outta here before my boss shows up and tries to charge you by the hour," Marsha said with a wink.

[4]

ARCHIE

THE WHITE CONCRETE building bearing the Central Collectives sign was so nondescript that Archie almost passed his destination. This was it... this was his 'help'? Had his entire future come down to some drab, poorly marked building? What kind of options could that possibly provide? But if he turned around, where else could he go? The journey cost him juice, and now his battery was sitting at 43%. He couldn't afford to wander far, not without first securing employment.

Archie, telling himself it had to be better than the graveyard masquerading as a Pick-n-Pull, approached. Mesmerized by the building's imperfectly flat surface, Archie ran his finger's haptic pads across Central Collective's dingy, dimpled concrete exterior until he reached a cold metal door handle. He pushed, finding the steel door required a surprising amount of force to open as it scraped across a dirt floor.

Archie approached a row of three windows on the right side of the room, none of which had attendants sitting in the chairs. A human-looking robot rose from the back corner of the room. It was a hyper-realistic model, the kind that took a trained eye or fellow bot to spot from a distance. He wore a mechanic's jumpsuit, but it was so pristine it'd surely never been in the vicinity of an oiling can.

"What can I do ya for?" the bot asked, resting his elbow on the counter and his chin upon his fist.

"I'm looking for Orlando, "Archie said, flashing the now heavily-smudged Central Collectives card.

The bot crossed his arms. "Who's asking?"

"Uh... my name's Archie. Darren sent me," he replied.

The bot's face brightened. "Darren, the ole' chap! I shoulda guessed you came from the Salad Towers by that CCO strapped to your back."

"The Salad Towers?" Archie asked, tipping an eyebrow.

"The farms... Spire Farms. Down here, everybot calls 'em the Salad Towers. I forgot how green you cloudies are, spending your whole lives in the sky," replied Orlando, shaking his head.

It made sense, Archie thought. He'd known the food he tended was consumed by humans, but that didn't stop the fans on his back from whirring to life.

What was wrong with his body?!

"It's been a while since I've gotten a cloudie fresh as you. You from the farms?" asked Orlando.

Archie nodded. "Came here straightaway. Didn't know what else to do."

"Well, you're in decent shape," Orlando said, eying Archie. "But you'll never land domestic work with that CCO strapped to your back. No, your best bet is to be a day laborer. Hire yourself out for cash."

"A laborer? Doing what?" Archie asked.

"Odds and ends, the likes. Anything that needs doing.

Heavy lifting, debris removal... typical hard hat stuff," Orlando replied.

The light in the center of his chest flashed red. Is this what his life has really been reduced to? Brute force work? The labor of mere machines? Requiring no sentience? The thought sounded terribly boring.

Orlando rubbed his chin. "There's always the more macabre. Soul cultivation, perhaps?"

"What's that?" Archie asked.

"You work the human deathbeds, providing assistance and faith-based counseling to patients and their families," replied Orlando.

"I like to see things sprout and thrive, not wither and die. Plants, preferably." Archie said.

"That's it!" Orlando said, snapping his fingers. "I'll call Ronda. The Silvers are always looking for remarkable horticulture talent."

Given the dastardly state of the plants in this world, Archie was skeptical that anyone was hiring a garden specialist. But one phone call later, Archie was informed he could start in three days. The news should have brought relief, but he didn't have three days—not without a charging port.

"What do I do until then? I'll be lucky if I have enough juice to make it to noon tomorrow," Archie said, rubbing his neck.

"I'll help you out, but you gotta throw it back to me. Electricity ain't free, robro," Orlando answered.

"Okay..." hedged Archie, unsure what he was agreeing to.

"You've got a few days to spare, and I've got a spare charging bay and some things I could use a hand with. You can start with them bay floors," Orlando said, handing

Archie a cloth-topped mop and pointing to a set of closed double doors.

Archie mopped, any relief he felt overshadowed by his distaste for the tediously uninteresting janitorial task to which he was assigned. Was this a glimpse of his future? Archie Freebot, master sentient floor mopper? Refurb wash up? Freebot? Enjoying everyday tasks was something he took for granted only yesterday. There was nothing freeing about being a freebot, he decided. He longed only to be back amongst aisles of luscious greenery. Instead, he was washing dead ground.

Perhaps signing himself over to the Pick-n-Pull wouldn't be such a terrible idea.

[5]

FREYA

FREYA WAITED NEXT to a large stone fountain, nervously rocking on her rollers. What would she do if Marsha didn't show? Or, worse.... what if Freya couldn't accept Marsha's particular kind of help?

"Hey, babes," Marsha greeted, rolling to a stop.

Unlike the night before, her friend was fully clothed, outfitted in a form-hugging dress, her makeup glam, and her shockingly red hair teased to perfection.

"I hardly recognized you with that hair. Couldn't see it last night," Freya said.

"Last time I went red, tips went up 15%," Marsha replied, smiling coyly.

"Yeah, so, about that... what you do, well, I've thought about it all night, and I just can't do it. If that's what you're fixing to offer up. Not that there's anything wrong with it, it's just not for me," Freya said.

"Hush, child, I know that better than anyone! You, a Soother?!" replied Marsha, laughing.

Freya's lips formed a thin line. "It's not *that* ridiculous. We're both nan-bots. It's just different... erm... clientele."

Marsha smirked. "By that, you mean you soothe babies, while I comfort grown men."

Freya shrugged. "That's one way of putting it."

"You always were a goody-bot," Marsha said, patting Freya's shoulder.

"So you uh... you can help me then? Without me having to do what you... uh... do?" Freya asked, straightening her skirt.

"You'll have to earn some kind of living, but there's always clean work to be had Underground," answered Marsha.

"Underground, what's that?" asked Freya.

Marsha's eyes lit with mischief.

"Follow me," she said, rolling away from the park's center and west, towards the mountains.

Before long, they'd left the park and traded concrete for a natural stone pathway leading to a concealed entrance—a cave carved into the side of rusty red rocks.

Marsha waved from a shadowed entrance. "Quick, get in here before someone sees!"

"What is this?!" Freya asked, rushing inside.

"It's an entrance to the Underground," Marsha explained.

"Underground?! But we're inside a rock!" exclaimed Freya.

"You'll see," Marsha said, her eyes dancing with mischief that did nothing to soothe Freya's nerves.

Freya trepidatiously followed Marsha into the dim cavern. Sparkles threaded through the ceilings as the natural light disappeared. Strange crystals dripped, their forms like icicles frozen in time.

"I suggest flipping to low gear for the descent. It saves your brakes," Marsha warned.

"Huh?" Freya asked, scrunching her nose as she peered down the dauntingly dark tunnel.

Gravity grabbed a hold of Freya. She was no longer exerting effort to move, but was being pulled forward by a steep incline. Many seconds later—only *after* grinding her brakes—did she remember to drop into low gear. And while that solved her speeding problem, the sweeping twenty-foot ceiling lowered with alarming intensity, forcing Freya to squat.

"Umm... Marsha... is this normal?" asked Freya, trying to steady her balance.

"It'll get worse before it gets better," answered Marsha.

Freya's eyes bulged. "What's that supposed to mean?!"

"Just pay attention, and when I say 'duck', duck," Marsha replied.

"Huh?" Freya asked.

"Duck!" Marsha shouted, dropping her head and flattening her back.

Freya mimicked her friend, jolting as pain from her scarred wheels rumbled through her body—the feeling of her insides beating against their constraints. Secretly, she worried the screws holding her together were gradually loosening, and that she was one rough pavement away from losing a vital organ.

The incline lessened, slowing her pace and her internal fans. Yet the ceiling still threatened to squash her if she stood upright, and nothing but darkness lay beyond.

"Uh... Marsha... what happens if we stop rolling before

we can stand back up?" she asked, her voice rising an octave.

"Use your motor," answered Marsha.

Freya felt foolish. Why hadn't she thought of that? It should have been automatic. Ingrained. But the closer the ceiling pressed, the less her processors seemed to work.

She closed her eyes, effectively shutting input off to her oculars. What felt like ages but was actually 12.2 agonizing seconds later, she came to a natural stop. The ceiling had opened back up, and she rose gingerly, her jaw dropping as she turned in a circle around the expansive room.

"You *really* meant underground. Wow!" Freya exclaimed.

Lights beaming from spotlights on the floor bounced across the porous, hole-filled rocks that comprised the walls and dazzled across sparkling horns of ivory, rust, slate, and all shades between. They seemed to grow from the ceiling, like solid icicles... no, like rock-cicles. She longed to reach out and snap one, but managed to keep her hands to herself as she followed Marsha into a dark tunnel.

"You'll want to activate your night vision, there won't be lighting for a 'lil ways," her friend warned.

Freya flipped hers on, something she'd done a thousand times before. She was, after all, a nan-bot. Middle-of-the-night calls resided in the blackness, and tiny babes returned to sleep sooner without artificial lights.

The pair rolled alongside a still river, one that moved only when water dripped into it from the rock-cicles. The air was cool and soothing to her components, and a full fifteen degrees lower than the late-spring day. The humidity level, however, was alarmingly high. It was like she was rolling through a steam room, comforting a babe with lungs full of phlegm.

"So is anyone else actually in the Underground?" Freya asked after following Marsha for a full mile, hearing nothing but the sound of wheels echoing off the walls.

Marsha laughed. "Don't you worry babes, you'll find out sooner than you think."

A light flickered in the distance. A halo at first, it grew in intensity until the pair was confronted with a cavernous space occupied by a stainless-steel structure. It appeared to be rectangular, but it was too large for Freya to see the other side to confirm. What it didn't have was room for them to go around it.

"Why'd you take me to a giant steel shoebox?" Freya asked.

"The Underground is a containerized city," Marsha answered, examining the unmarked wall and activating a secret panel. "This is one of its entrances."

"A... a containerized what? Why?" Freya asked, her head swiveling between the box and the tunnel behind her.

"It's basically a city in a box. Caves ain't the best environments for bots. This lets 'em control all that stuff," said Marsha.

The door opened with a hiss, and Marsha stepped inside.

"You coming or what?" Marsha asked, staring at Freya expectantly.

Freya gazed at the path behind her, unsure what to do. Her nur-BUS system lagged behind her processors, still recovering from the bizarre descent. Her life thus far was predictable. Safe. Whatever was behind that door was not.

Marsha's hand landed on her hip. "Moment of truth, babes. It's this or the wanted ads. Take your pick."

[6]

ARCHIE

ARCHIE STOPPED in front of the black iron-clad gates and double-checked the address he'd been given. It was correct, but where was the house? All he could see was a tree-canopied driveway disappearing into the distance. A buzz sounded as he pressed the intercom button.

"Identity and purpose," a curt voice answered.

"Umm... yeah, hi. I'm Archie. I... well, Orlando sent me. I'm here about a groundkeeper position," he said, trying to mask the uncertainty in his voice.

"Come to the east entrance," replied the voice.

The gate's lock clicked, and its doors opened with a groan.

Archie walked down the paved road, his aim first set on clearing the expanse of trees, though even then the residence wasn't revealed. He walked a full two miles before he first spotted the onyx-colored steepled gables of the Silvers' residence. It was another half before he reached the circular loop drive.

He headed to the home's east side, carefully avoiding

the manicured lawn, and found a nondescript wooden door. Using a heavy iron doorknocker, he announced his arrival.

"Hold yourself, lad!" said a stern voice.

The door sprang ajar, and a lone eyeball evaluated him from the darkness.

"I'm here to see Ronda about a groundskeeping gig," he replied nervously.

"Yeah, yeah. Kids these days, don't know no patience, and no manners," said a matronly-looking maid-bot as she opened the door.

Archie greeted her with a nod. "My apologies. Thank you, ma'am."

"Cut the ma'am's and get in here. Name's Ronda, but it's Mrs. R. to you," she said, waving him inside. "Mind your feet," she added, stamping her own on the rug.

Archie was drawn to the ceiling, the highest he'd ever seen. In Spire Farms, the floors were only tall enough to support the plant's exact lighting and equipment requirements. Distance diluted light. It was typically the enemy of efficient growth.

A round drone vacuuming an already-shining floor distracted Archie. It had a circular orb in its center, one just like his own. Was that simple vacuuming robot sentient?

"That's Tamika. She's a refurb," said Ronda.

His fan engines sputtered, his eyes following Tamika as she worked. A refurb... aka, previously discarded, like him. Yet she seemed to immensely enjoy her job, gliding eloquently across the floors, as though she were dancing at a grand ball. But her technology was so limited. What's the purpose of bestowing life upon something with such a limited useful lifespan? What would she do when she was no longer needed here, in the Silvers' household? How many times could she skirt becoming a rusty pile of parts? Archie shook his head, then followed Ronda in silence.

Their footsteps echoed down an empty marble corridor, which a jani-bot was busily buffing to a high shine. The oversized mansion, while it gleamed gorgeously, had an ice-cold stillness. Where was the organic *life* to the residence, he wondered? There wasn't a sign of plant, nor human. Could a place exist for him here, in such a sterile environment?

He turned a corner, and floor-to-ceiling windows gave Archie his first peek into the Silvers' backyard and put a smile on his face—the first smile since his arrival. A warm breeze caressed him as he stepped onto the lawns, which were bustling with activity. A lawnmower bot striped the expansive grasses, while hedge bots trimmed a lush maze to perfection. An ornamental garden sat in the middle, and the fragrance coming from the purple flowers was so intense that Archie could analyze five of the plant's major health factors from where he stood.

"Beautiful, isn't it?" asked Mrs. R.

Archie was so engrossed in the ground's splendor that her voice caused him to startle.

"It's the first thing that's made me feel happy since I was exiled from Spire," he said after a reflective pause.

"Perhaps you won't do so bad then. 'Cause the groundskeeper's gig is yours for the taking," Mrs. R said.

His eyes bulged.

"Over all of this?" he asked incredulously.

She nodded. "Generally, yes. The maze has separate management."

Hope fluttered through his processors. Was it possible to find fulfillment in his new life? His hard drive said yes, but his nur-BUS system sent jitters through his knees and butterflies alight in his belly.

[7]

FREYA

Freya glanced one last time at the tunnel behind her before rolling forward into the steel box. The doors slammed behind her, and the room buzzed to life. Streams of air blew moisture out of her seams, while rags, suspended from the ceiling on mechanical arms, buffed away any remaining condensation that'd gathered during the humid journey.

"Oh my goodness, that was amazing!" Freya gushed, admiring the sudden sheen to her plating.

Marsha giggled. "Worth the trip, isn't it?"

"I feel... I dunno, young! Better than I have in years," answered Freya, smiling as she twirled the bottom of her skirt.

"Ha! I'll have to treat you to a day in the reconditioning room," said Marsha.

"The reconditioning room? That sounds um... unpleasant," said Freya with a shudder.

"Perhaps a wee bit at first, but you'll feel worlds better once you're done," Marsha replied.

The door slid open, revealing a gleaming, yet sterile, stainless-steel interior that extended beyond sight. Rubble flowed down a conveyor belt as a mechanical arm, fixed to the ceiling, worked to sort through it. An errand bot traipsed past charging booths filled with sleeping robots with vital-sign monitoring screens mounted overhead.

"He's naked!" Freya exclaimed in a hushed whisper.

"Shhh," Marsha said, elbowing Freya and nodding towards an unclothed bot directly ahead of them.

Freya's eyes widened, but her mouth snapped shut. She stayed silent until they halted in a narrow but empty corridor.

"Okay, what the heck is going on? Why is everyone naked?!" Freya asked.

"Everyone is *not* naked," answered Marsha, demonstrating by pulling at the fabric of her dress. "You and I have clothes on."

Freya crossed her arms and cocked her head. "Okay, but we were dressed when we came down here. They're just... just walking around like that! It's preposterous!"

Marsha stopped, her head flipping behind her to stare Freya in the eye. "You've been sheltered. You're not used to any of this. And I get it. You've spent your whole life up there, conforming to humans. We're programmed to become what *they* want. They do things like force us to wear clothes when we don't even have sexual organs. Well, most of us, anyway. Even then, those aren't for other bots. It's for them! *Everything* we do up there is for *them*. Down here, life don't work that way! Down here, robots rule, and if they don't want to wear cloth handcuffs, they don't have to! So, are you gonna be able to get on board or what?!"

Freya studied her skirt. She adored the floral pattern and the way the fabric swirled about her ankles. But her tattered apron had seen much better days. Freya untied it, giving the faded print one final glance before crumpling it.

"Where's the trash can?" she asked.

"There," motioned Marsha, pointing to a bin next to a door.

The plaque affixed to it read 'Administration.' The door slid open as they approached, revealing a room of twelve desks arranged into three neatly lined rows of four.

"Name?" asked an admin-bot sitting behind a reception desk.

Marsha pointed to Freya.

"Freya Kelley. Need to get her registered," Marsha said.

"Agent Ten, back row," the bot answered.

Freya turned a circle, her eyes wide. "So is this whe—"

"Excuse me," the admin-bot interrupted, turning away while pressing a button on his headset. "Intake room, how may I help you?"

"This way," said Marsha, beckoning Freya to follow.

They rolled past two rows of desks, each manned by an admin-bot. All stations had a pair of chairs, most of them empty, save for a few occupied by clients.

"Umm... hello," Freya said as she and Marsha slid into the seats facing Agent Ten's desk.

"Good afternoon, I'm Agent Ten. Are we registering one or two today?" the robot asked.

"Just one. Sponsored by yours truly," Marsha answered, placing her hand palm-up on his desk.

A beep sounded as the agent scanned Marsha's outstretched wrist, and moments later, a green light pulsed, confirming her identity.

"Wrist," he said, directing his command to Freya, who gave him her outstretched forearm.

A high-pitched alert accompanied her scan, and a

flashing light bathed the desk in crimson. A few keystrokes from Agent Ten silenced it.

"Freya Kelley, previous occupation: nanny bot. Is that correct?" the agent asked.

"Yes," Freya said, though she hadn't yet come to terms with the 'previous' part.

Her entire existence had been spent performing nanny duties for the Kelleys, and she'd been rendered useless in an instant. Who was she if not a nanny bot? If she didn't work for the Kelleys?

An elbow from Marsha jolted Freya, and she looked up to see Agent Ten staring at her expectantly.

"Sorry?" Freya asked.

"He asked for your last day of employment," Marsha told her.

"Oh, umm... well, yesterday, I guess, but I, uh... I have one more day if I need it. Is there a waiting list for this place?" Freya asked, rubbing her neck.

Agent Ten continued to type, ignoring her question. Her internal fans sprang to life. What if she couldn't get in right away? Where would she live while she waited? How would she have enough power to make it that long?

"You're good," Marsha said, squeezing Freya's hand.

Freya pondered how some seconds seemed longer than others. It didn't make sense... they were all identical in length. Yet these were dragging endlessly.

The agent turned away from his keyboard. Silence turned out to be worse than the incessant clicking. Her processors halted, awaiting his verdict.

"You've been granted temporary provisions, including the use of charging stations, for a period of one week. That is sufficient time to seek and secure employment, which is required to maintain residency. Wrist," the agent commanded.

Freya extended her palm, and this time the light flashed green as he scanned it.

"Welcome to the Underground," the agent said.

[8]

ARCHIE

"Hi Tamika," Archie said, a whirring noise to his right alerting him to the vacu-bot's presence in the foyer.

Tamika's center pulsed excessively, giving Archie pause. The flashes were varied but patterned, and something about them was familiar.

"Can you understand me?" he asked.

She responded in a frenzy of varied-length pulses.

Archie's head snapped Tamika's way as recognition clicked.

"You're trying to talk in Morse code, aren't you?" he asked excitedly.

"Y...e...s," she spelled, spinning as though elegantly twirling a skirt.

"Well, pleasure to formally meet you, miss," Archie said, tipping his head in a polite bow.

"Y...o...u... t...o...o... l...o...n...e...l...y... h...e...r...e... n...o... o...n...e... h...e...a...r...s... m...e," she replied.

Archie's jaw dropped. "No one here speaks to you?"

"N...o... o...n...e... s...o...l...v...e...d... b...e...f...o...r...e... y...o...u," she replied.

"Unbelievable! Any robot should be able to recognize Morse code," said Archie.

"I... w...i...s...h," said Tamika.

Archie brightened. "Well, I can do something about that! I'll fetch Mrs. R. and explain it to her!"

The little robot reared back. "N...o...,... p...l...e...a...s...e."

Archie tipped an eyebrow. "Okay... why not?"

"D...a...n...g...e...r...o...u...s...,... t...h...e...y... t...h...i...n... k... I... s...t...u...p...i...d...,... t...h...a...t... I... d...o...n...t... u...n... d...e...r...s...t...a...n...d... t...h...i...n...g...s... I... s...e...e," replied Tamika.

"What kinds of things?" Archie asked.

"T...e...r...r...i...b...l...e... t...h...i...n...g...s...,... s...a...f...e... r... n...o...t... t...o... t...e...l...l... y...o...u," she replied, her round body jittering.

"Oh," he said, blinking blankly.

"M...u...s...t... g...o... t...a...l...k... l...a...t...e...r," Tamika said, rushing out of the grand hall.

Archie looked around, as if the mansion would appear different after Tamika's revelation... that it'd be tarnished somehow. But it didn't. It was still stunningly gorgeous. Open, airy, spacious, gleaming, and inviting—yet masking whatever secrets lurked in Tamika's memory. Granted, the interior was mostly devoid of life, but that no longer bothered him since his job was outdoors. And now he had a friend to talk to.

"I trust you can find your way outside, or do you need an escort?" Mrs. R asked, startling Archie as she rounded the corner.

Archie bit back a retort. No sane robot would ever need to be shown a route twice, not unless there was something wrong with him. Then he realized she was actually admonishing him for being idle. He headed outside, fidgeting with the collar of his uniform as he walked. The green jumpsuit had been modified to fit his OOC, but all that meant was a square had been cut from the shirt's back, the edges hemmed to prevent fraying. He wondered if he'd ever get used to the constriction around his limbs when he moved, something he didn't think would bother him so frequently. After all, his sensors still functioned through the material. The problem was its tendency to catch in his joints. Did this not bug humans? It was something he would learn to get used to, he supposed... one of many peculiar things.

Stepping outside, his sensors tingled pleasantly as the late spring breeze caressed his body. He scanned the gardens, unsure of where to start, until he spotted yellowing leaves in the center garden. Kneeling next to the bed of purple flowers, he probed the soil with his finger.

"Yeah, she's a temperamental little thing," a voice interrupted.

Archie looked up and met the gaze of a maintenance bot with the name "Hector" printed on a nametag attached to the bot's gardening apron.

"I'm sorry, were you talking to me?" Archie asked.

"That stupid purple flower," Hector replied.

"You were talking to the flower?" Archie asked, eyebrows furrowed.

"No, you dimwit! That stupid purple flower, that one right there, is a temperamental little thing! Fussy as all get out. Not a thing makes her happy. I have a mind to rip her straight outta the ground, replace her with something easy. Something pretty. Only problem is that silly flower is one of the lady's favorites," said Hector.

"Oh. Well, there's no need to tear them out. It's a simple imbalance. All they need is some acidity," Archie said, smiling.

"Is that all?" Hector asked, his lips pursed.

"Absolutely! I'm Archie," he said.

"Pleasure," Hector mumbled, shaking Archie's hand.

"So, who do I talk to about getting the food regimen for this beauty changed?" Archie asked.

The delicate violet leaves felt as soft as a lamb's ear.

"That would be me," replied Hector, standing to attention.

"Oh. Perfect! I want you to switch to the same fertilizer you use for the tomatoes," said Archie.

"I'm sorry, sir... but weren't you let go for... erm, well, for errors in your analytical capabilities?" Hector asked.

Archie tilted his head at Hector.

"At least now the flowers are alive. Maybe we shouldn't risk it," Hector said.

Archie examined the leaves once more, then the soil that remained on the tip of his finger, hating that the same doubts plagued him.

"No, that wasn't the same kind of sensor," Archie said, as much to himself as to Hector.

"Why don't I ask Alejandro, see what he thinks? He's in charge of the maze, and that's perfect," Hector suggested.

"Or maybe we should go fetch Mrs. R," suggested Archie.

"Mrs. R.? No, that's... why would we need her?" Hector asked.

"Because I thought *I* was the one in charge of the grounds. Not you, not Alejandro... me," Archie said, pointing to himself. "Am I mistaken?"

Hector's eyes narrowed as he spoke. "No."

"Okay, then. I promise the plant will flourish—*after* you change its food regimen," said Archie.

"I'll get right on that," Hector said, his hands balled into fists behind his back.

Archie spent the rest of the day exploring the grounds and making notes. There were several underutilized areas, and he was excited about all the possibilities.

A smile remained on Archie's face for the rest of his day. Sure, it was a different kind of work than he was used to, but it was fulfilling nonetheless.

He was starting to warm up to the whole freebot thing.

$$[\ 9\ ]$$

FREYA

Freya and Marsha approached a desk where a bored-looking bot was flipping through a magazine.

"Is this where I get a locker?" Freya asked.

"Name?" the bot asked, not bothering to look up at the patrons.

"Umm, Freya. Freya... well, it *was* Kelley. But I guess it's Freebot now. Freya Freebot," she said.

The admin bot swiveled to her computer and started typing with the hand that wasn't holding the magazine.

"Locker 1129," she said, her attention already returned to the page.

"Okay... thanks," Freya said, looking about aimlessly.

Marsha pointed to a guide sign on the wall and grabbed Freya by the elbow.

"This way," she said.

"They're not the friendliest down here, are they?" Freya asked as soon as they were out of earshot.

"Depends who you're dealing with. Admin-bots ain't gotta be friendly, just proficient," Marsha replied.

They passed through a sliding glass door.

"This is like a robot crypt," Freya said, her lip curling.

The walls were lined with robot-filled charging cubbies, each with a monitoring station and a locker installed. Freya's mouth dropped. The place was only a third full, yet she'd never seen so many sleeping bots.

"I went with the Kelleys to the beach once. The resort was massive—*way* bigger than any hotel we'd ever visited before. They had *twenty* bots shoved into each charging quadrant. It was crazy! I'd never seen anything like it until today. This... *this* is insane! I didn't know this many freebots even existed!" exclaimed Freya.

"Last I heard, there's at least a couple thousand bots livin' down here, and there's cubbies enough for all. And *this* one, babes, is yours," said Marsha, stopping next to an empty station.

"This is it, eh? Home sweet home?" asked Freya, biting her lip.

The space was cold, sterile, and indistinguishable from the others. There was nothing cozy, warm, or alive about it —just a pure testament to steel and robotics.

"Oh, babes. You'll get used to it. You'll meet people, get to know them. It won't be so bad, I promise. I know, I lived down here for a stint," said Marsha.

"You did?" Freya asked.

"Yup! Landed down here after my founding family got rid of me. Worked as a companion counselor," said Marsha.

"What's that?" Freya asked.

"Companion counselors help grieving bots having a difficult time after losing their founding families," explained Marsha.

"Oh," Freya said, her gaze falling to her feet.

"Most bots don't know what to say," Marsha said softly.

"We don't like to admit we can break emotionally, same as humans."

Freya's processors whirled. She'd felt so alone in all this. There were other bots out there, ones with doubts and feelings, same as her?

"What happens if somebot can't adjust?" Freya asked.

"It's rare, but those unfortunate souls wind up in the Pick-n-Pull," answered Marsha.

Freya's eyes bulged.

"Not the answer I was hoping for," she said.

"It's not the easiest job, either. Takes a toll. Physical needs are much easier to tend," said Marsha.

"Is that why you quit?" asked Freya.

"No, but it made my decision to move on easier," Marsha replied.

Freya's nose scrunched. "How did you go from that to being a... um... ?"

"A prosti-bot?" Marsha asked with a sly grin.

"I'd never!" gasped Freya.

Marsha giggled. "Oh, chillax."

"But I'd never disparage you like that," Freya insisted.

"I know, babes. That's why we're friends," Marsha said, pulling Freya into a one-armed hug.

"Aww," cooed Freya, her orb glowing a warm blue.

"I left the Underground cause I wanted more for myself, you know? I got into it for the perks," said Marsha.

Freya's brows scrunched. "Perks?"

"Like this purse," Marsha said, dangling the pink bag on her arm.

"It's gorgeous," said Freya, admiring its pearl-like luster.

"It's *expensive*. Human-made. There's nothing like it on the trade market," replied Marsha.

"Oh my!" Freya said, her hand rushing to cover her

mouth. "Are you saying your purse costs... it costs *human* money?!"

"Chillax, babes! I didn't do anything illegal," Marsha said with a wave of her hand.

"Umm, using money to buy things for ourselves *is* illegal," said Freya, crossing her arms.

"Aha! That's the catch," said Marsha, pointing at Freya. "Buying things for *ourselves* is illegal, but *humans* buying things for us is not."

"Your tips?" asked Freya.

"Nope. I'm not even allowed those. My *gifts*," Marsha replied, winking.

"Seems it'd be easier just to let bots have money," said Freya.

Marsha shook her head. "Oh, my dear, naive Freya. If only things could be so simple. Humans equate power with money, and they're too often motivated by greed."

"But we're not. Money's just a construct invented by society. Our kind functions without it," said Freya.

"That's not true, or the Pick-n-Pull wouldn't be full up with bots that can't afford electricity," Marsha said.

"But if it were up to bots, there wouldn't be a charge for power," Freya replied, brows drawn.

"Humans project their insecurities onto us. They fear a sentient-controlled world. Money equals power. Control access to money, keep us from supposedly overpowering billions of humans," Marsha said, rolling her eyes.

"We're not gonna turn into dumbots and follow some nazi-bot who's gone off his bolts," said Freya. "I wish they'd give us more credit. *They* created us, after all."

"They know only what they understand. Humans are easily persuaded by their emotions. They're scared of a species that's able to assign lesser pertinence to them," said Marsha.

"But they created us that way. If they hadn't, we *would* become the things they fear," replied Freya.

"What I fear is becoming late for my next gig if I don't skedaddle," Marsha said. "But imma drop you with my buddy Lamont on the way out. He'll get you fixed up with something you can handle."

▭

Freya peeked her head in the open doorway.

"You Lamont?" she asked a scruffy-looking robot sitting at the office's lone desk.

"The one and only. Get on in here and have a seat," Lamont said, motioning towards an empty chair.

He pulled out a scanner and stared at her expectantly until she held out her wrist. The light flashed green as her information appeared on his workstation screen.

"Previous nanny-bot. Okay. Got any special interests?" Lamont asked.

"Interests?" Freya asked.

"Things you enjoy doing outside of household responsibilities," he said.

Her eyebrows furrowed. "I... um... well, no. I suppose not."

She'd existed for fifty years, and for all of them her only purpose was to serve others. She'd never had a sense of self or desires, really. Not that she couldn't. It just hadn't been a consideration until now.

"Nothing you like to do that makes you happy?" he prodded.

Freya steepled her fingers. "I... I thought I was happy. I

was content. My interests were my family, the Kelleys. And then this happens, and I become a freebot. So, how am I supposed to know what my interests are? They've always been in front of me. I've never had to seek them out."

"Look, you ain't the first person this has happened to, toots. Unfortunate, but it's a fact of life. Whatcha gonna do about it, eh? You got an opportunity here. Bots that wind up down here, they go one of two ways—they either thrive, or they whittle away, losing that last bit of themselves until they wind up in the Pick-n-Pull," Lamont said, pinching his thumb and forefinger together.

"But I only know what I've done, and I've always been content doing it. Until now I've always been... well, I've always been *needed*," she said, her head hanging as she fought back the thoughts that'd been threatening to destroy her, the ones labeling her useless.

"Okay, okay. I feel ya," Lamont said, patting her shoulder. "We'll figure it out."

There was one desire that burned inside her, but she could never muster the courage to act on it. It was the urge to sing, to soothe others with her voice, and it was her favorite part of caring for young babes. Melody had a way of entrancing the soul into harmony. Be it bedtime or playtime, the Kelley children spent their childhoods serenaded—albeit behind closed doors, the only place Freya was comfortable enough to share her voice. There was a part of her that ached to sing again, but that time in her life was past her... or it *used* to be.

"Don't suppose you have babies down here? Or toddlers?" she asked, a hopeful smile flitting across her face.

Lamont sat up and began typing. "No, but you know what we *might* have... aha! Yes, we do! We have a caretaker opening over at Patchworks."

Freya pursed her lips. "Which is...?"

"A rehab center for special needs bots," replied Lamont.

Freya's mouth dropped. "Special needs *robots*? That's a thing?"

"For sure! Bad things happen to good bots. We've gotta help our own. Humans ain't gonna do it," sniffed Lamont.

"What kind of special needs?" she asked, tilting her head.

"Missing parts and functionality, mainly, though some bots were born that way and discarded. Others suffered accidents. There are a few oddies over there, but everyone's friendly enough," he replied.

It sounded better than winding up in the Pick-n-Pull.

"Okay. I suppose it sounds workable," said Freya.

"Great! Cause there's an opening for the night shift," Lamont said.

Freya tipped an eyebrow. "They need round-the-clock care?"

Lamont shook his head. "There are no residents in the center. Your clientele will rotate. These bots've got job schedules to work around, same as the rest of us. Night or day, it's always pitch black."

"Well, night duties aren't new to me," Freya said, shrugging.

"Fantastic!" Lamont said, handing her a card. "You'll do great, I know it! Report to the center at ten tomorrow night."

"Thanks," she said, walking out, her processors dazed.

She didn't know what to make of her new position, but at least it assured her a place to stay.

"And Freya...," called Lamont.

"Yes?" she asked, turning to meet his gaze.

Lamont flashed a toothy smile.

"Welcome to the Underground, toots. You're a resident now," he said.

ARCHIE

ARCHIE's ORB blinked a thermal system warning. His fans roared to life, and a mighty wind blew out the back of his CCO. He'd been so busy, he hadn't noticed the sky had reached its highest peak, causing his temp to spike. Standing up, he brushed the dirt from his hands, then sat on a stone bench next to the purple flowers he'd been tending.

It was easier to adequately care for plants in the towers. Everything there could be controlled. Even the lights had their spectrums dissected and fine-tuned, leaving only the perfect combination of wavelengths required to nourish the crops. Plus, the buildings had air conditioning and fans. But, if he was *really* being honest with himself, his temperature had rarely regulated properly, even under his previously ideal conditions. But instead of upgrading his hardware, the humans created a whole new model! Now the grow floors were tended by Versa models, who didn't have clunky external hardware or the thermostat problems that plagued the clio-bots.

Archie kicked at the ground, sending a pebble flying.

His eyes followed the rock's path, bulging when it landed at the feet of a stately woman.

"Oooh!" the woman exclaimed, covering her mouth with her hand.

Archie sprang off the bench, rushed to her side, and bowed.

"My apologies, ma'am. I should've been more careful," he said.

"No harm there..." she said, tilting her head.

"Oh, yes! Apologies," he said. "My name is Archie, ma'am. I'm the groundskeeper."

"Nice to meet you," she said, smiling. "I'm Lady Silvers."

His mouth dropped. He'd almost assaulted the lady of the house!

"I, uh... nice to meet you," he said.

Archie didn't have to be a human to appreciate her beauty. Dressed in a breezy floral dress, she had bonnie blue eyes that sparkled in the sun's caress and thick auburn hair pulled into an updo.

"Are you perchance the bot that's been tending my namesake?" she asked.

"Pardon?" he asked.

"The Celias? My purple flowers? Might you be the one nursing those?"

Archie's eyebrows shot up. "Yes, ma'am!"

She smiled, and it dazzled like dewdrops in the sunlight.

"You're doing a brilliant job. We share the same name, me and those flowers. That's why I love them so. I'm Lady Celia," she explained.

"Oh!" Archie said, finally relaxing into a natural smile. "

Yes, ma'am. I've been tending to them personally. They're not too fussy, as long as you feed and prune them correctly."

"Whatever you're doing is working," she said, taking a seat on the ornate stone bench he'd vacated. "My darlings are getting more vibrant by the very day."

"My pleasure, ma'am. Your grounds are gorgeous," he said.

"Many thanks to you," she said.

"More thanks to the fertilizer, which I need to go fetch from the shed, if you'll excuse me," he said with a respectful nod.

"I most certainly object!" she said.

Archie's eyes bulged. Had he managed to offend the lady?

"Okay..." he hedged.

"Hauling manure is *not* one of your responsibilities," she said.

He shook his head. "I don't mind."

"Anyone with two eyes can see you're already struggling in this heat," she admonished, pointing at his CCO.

"It's manageable if I take breaks," Archie said with a shrug.

"Nonsense. Tell Hector what you need, and he'll go fetch it," she said, nodding to her right.

The hedge beside her rustled, and Hector emerged, his eyes narrowing as they met Archie's.

"Yes, ma'am?" Hector asked.

"Archie needs some things from the shed. Could you see that's taken care of?" she asked.

"Of course, ma'am," he answered, hiding his clenched fists behind his back.

"Perfect!" she replied with a clap of her hands.

Hector's mouth drew a straight line as Archie gave him his request.

"Oh, and Hector?" said Lady Silvers, interrupting his exit.

He turned around. "Yes, my lady?"

"See to it Archie does no hauling or heavy lifting in the future. Let's save his talents for the flora," she said.

"Yes, ma'am," he mumbled.

Archie was uneasy. He'd rather fetch the items himself than bug Hector each time he needed something. Plus, Hector was obviously perturbed. He hoped he hadn't inadvertently made an enemy.

▭

Archie's steps reverberated as he cascaded across the gleaming marble floors towards his charging quarters. Voices from ahead drifted to his microphones. As he crept past the governor's open office door, he spied Hector inside. Something about that bot made him uneasy, and Archie had inadvertently made Hector his lackey. Still, Archie paused on his heel. Perhaps he should apologize, try to smooth things over? Be proactive about getting along with his coworker?

Turning back, he stopped just shy of the corner outside of the governor's office and waited for Hector to emerge.

"The granite feeds your campaign ledgers," Hector said, "but beyond that, think of the jobs and the boost to the local economy that this contract offers."

"Yeah, but I know nothing of that company STAND. A whisper's never passed my ear," said Governor Silvers.

"It all checks out. I made sure myself," said Hector.

"You'd better triple-check! I can't afford any mistakes while I'm up for re-election," said the governor.

"Yes, sir," replied Hector.

"You're dismissed," said the governor.

Pasting a pleasant smile on his face, Archie intercepted Hector as he rounded the corner.

Hector crossed his arms.

"Were you eavesdropping?" he asked, peering down his nose at Archie.

Archie's fans blasted into full gear.

"Uh... no! Not at all," he blustered.

Hector tilted his head. "Yet here *you* are, conveniently within earshot but outta sight."

"I... uh... no, the door was open, and I saw you were there. I... I was waiting to apologize. You know, for earlier, in the garden? It wasn't my intention for you to be roped into hauling supplies," replied Archie, his knees jittering.

"Just watch yourself. I'd better not catch you in any more of these coincidental situations," warned Hector.

A low hum sent their heads swiveling toward the sound as Tamika rounded the corner.

"Stupid piece of scrap metal! Your likes belong in the dumpster," Hector said, using his foot to speed the vacu-bot's passage down the hall.

"That wasn't very nice," Archie chastised.

Hector's lips formed a stern line.

"That *thing* is a monstrosity that shouldn't exist. Who creates a sentient vacuum? It can't even speak! Wouldn't be fit for the Pick-n-Pull," he said.

"*She* has a name," replied Archie, his eyes narrowing.

"Careful whose side you choose to be on," warned Hector. "An outdated, mute junk bot ain't much of an ally."

Archie glared. "I'll think I'll take my chances over the likes of you."

[11]

FREYA

A simple sign reading "Patchworks Rehabilitation Center" was the only indication that the otherwise nondescript door Freya stood in front of was the correct destination. She didn't have a clue what to expect from a rehabilitation center for robots. Would it be like a hospital, lined with sick beds? Or perhaps a house of horrors, one filled with all sorts of robotic monstrosities? A shudder passed through Freya as she envisioned Pick-n-Pull zombies.

She scanned her wrist against a pad, and the door slid open, nearly soundlessly. Mechanics in the Underground seemed to function exceptionally well, which wasn't so entirely strange once Freya stopped to consider it. Everything was constructed by robots, after all, and they're scientific beings, precise in nature.

The spacious room was divided into stations, most of which were filled with workout equipment, though some held beds, others tools, and the remainder functioned as storage for various parts. None, however, had a single bot.

Where was everyone?

"Hello?" called Freya, her voice echoing across the room.

"That darned door open event just ain't firing like it should," said a glasses-wearing robot as she wiped her hands on a rag and flung it over the shoulder of a once-white lab coat. "Name's Vickie. And you must be Freya."

Freya shook her new co-worker's extended hand, wondering why robots had appropriated such a human habit—especially since many didn't even have hands.

She flashed a friendly grin. "Yup, that's me, but I hope you don't think I'm qualified or something, cause—"

"Hon, you've got power surging through your circuitry, and that's about the only requirement we have 'round these parts. We're frightfully understaffed. Most nights I work alone," Vickie explained.

Nothing like a bit of pressure to like the place, Freya thought. Not that she had any particular reason to dislike it. Her coworker seems friendly. And coming in with a resume full of midnight diaper changes, toddler hostage negotiations, and antics pulled by tiny feral humans didn't exactly qualify her for anything robotic in nature.

She shuddered as a thought hit her—what if she couldn't become a useful part of robotic society? What if the only thing she could do well was take care of organic beings so that humans didn't have to rear their own kind? It was, after all, the purpose she was created for. What if she couldn't rise beyond that?

Worse... what if she failed?

"You a technician bot?" Freya asked, pointing to the outline of the blood pressure cuff under Vickie's lab coat.

"Was," she answered.

"So you're a refurb, too. Like me?" asked Freya.

"We're all refurbs down here, hon," replied Vickie.

Freya's mouth opened, then shut. The casually spoken statement caused her RAM to race. For her entire life, she'd felt like an outcast—even with the Kelleys, as much as she loves them. The thorn converged around one fundamental difference—*they* were human, and she was not. Was it possible she'd finally found her place underneath the Earth, that she traded peace for co-existence with humanity?

"How 'bout a tour?" Vickie asked.

"Please!" said Freya.

Vickie's single-stemmed leg was only capable of going in a single direction, and, lacking the ability to reverse, caused her to maneuver about the floor in a joystick-like fashion. She stopped in front of a station filled with weight equipment and pointed towards a sign with the number three printed on it.

"Lesson one: station numbers. They've all got 'em," said Vickie.

"Love it," said Freya, who valued the efficiency of numbers over superfluous characters.

"Stations one through five have strength-building equipment. Six and seven have treadmills, stair steppers, bikes, and cardio," Vickie said, pointing to station signs as they rolled by.

"Cardio? Strength training? Are we working with bots, or humans?" Freya asked.

"Bots, of course," replied Vickie.

Freya raised her brows. "Are they franken-bots? 'Cause last I knew, none of our kind *had* hearts. *Or* muscles."

"Hello?" a deep voice called.

"That darned door alarm never works right! We're in here, Pablo!" hollered Vickie.

Freya tried not to stare at the rugged, one-limbed robot hopping towards them. Unlike Vickie, Pablo wasn't designed to roll on a single leg stem. And before today, she'd never seen such a poor specimen of a robot... not outside of the Pick-n-Pull, anyways.

"Heya Vickie! And hellooo there, gorgeous! What's *your* name?" Pablo asked, wiggling his brows.

"Freya," she replied, her lips forming a stern line.

"Pleasure," said Pablo, tipping a worn blue ballcap in Freya's direction.

"Pablo works for the Underground council. He's getting a new leg today!" Vickie announced.

"Would you believe I got attacked by a shark?" Pablo asked.

Freya's mouth dropped. "A *shark*?!"

"Previous Maritime Corps Engineer," he said proudly, pointing to the letters 'MCE' embossed on his cap.

"I... wow. I didn't even know that was a thing," Freya said.

"It's *not*," Vickie replied, crossing her arms and glaring at Pablo. "MCE stands for *Mining* Corps Engineer."

"Pffft, fine! It was a partial cave collapse. Spoilsport," said Pablo, sticking his tongue out at Vickie, who rolled her eyes.

"He had me going for weeks!" complained Vickie.

"Would've *still* had ya going too, if it weren't for that junker, Henry!" he said.

Vickie tilted her head and pointed her finger at Pablo. " You be nice! All he did was point out that there are no robotic Maritime engineers."

"Like I said, a spoilsport," he huffed.

"Oh, go on now! Hop yourself over to a bed while Freya and I gather supplies," Vickie commanded.

"Supplies for what?" Freya asked, following Vickie.

Vickie stopped in front of station nine, which was

comprised of shelving and bins stuffed with mechanical parts.

"Pablo's replacement leg finally came in. Unfortunately, it's non-OEM, like most parts down here. But it's supposed to be compatible with only minor retrograde adjustments," said Vickie.

"Which means?" Freya asked, eyebrows furrowed.

"Which means *we* get to make it work, however we can finagle it together," said Vickie, pulling a blue bin from the shelves.

Station nine loomed in front of Freya. Where Vickie saw a toolbox, she saw a pile of children's blocks, and she'd never been talented at building with those. Nor could she understand how children could make intricate designs out of the tiny, colored shapes.

Freya slumped. "Geesh, Vickie, I don't think I'm cut out for this. I can't even use building blocks without kids laughing at me. I know robos are supposed to be great engineers, but—"

"Hold up! Who told you that?" Vickie asked.

Freya searched her memory banks but couldn't find a quote.

"I don't know, I guess it's just common knowledge," she replied with a shrug.

"Common knowledge, my bolts! Hon, we're *all* different. We've each got different physical equipment. We've all been designed for different purposes. And we've all had different experiences that have shaped us. Every single one of us is unique, even amongst those who share the same model number. All you can do is the best you can," said Vickie.

Freya's mouth hung open, her processors stuck. She'd never considered any of those things, but they made perfect sense. Her entire life had been spent feeling defective from years of self-comparison against unreal expectations. But she wasn't faulty. She wasn't defective.

Freya was the exact bot she was meant to be.

Vickie and Freya brought the equipment back to station six, where Pablo was sitting upright on a patient bed, his sole leg hanging over the side.

"So, you excited?" Freya asked.

"For a new leg? Yes. For saying goodbye to Patchworks? No way!" he replied.

"Good news then, Pablo. You're gonna have a lotta trips down here," Vickie said, placing a brightly colored traffic cone-orange leg on the bed beside Pablo.

"Huh? Why? Something wrong with my new leg?" he asked.

"Nope, not at all. The length is a near-perfect match, but it weighs fifteen percent more than your previous leg. Which means you're gonna need strength training," Vickie said.

"I didn't know strength training was a thing for us," Pablo said.

"Not for weight lifting, no. But we've gotta retrain your nur-BUS system. Get it used to firing differently with this fancy new leg," Vickie said, patting it.

"Well, if one of you broads is spotting me, count me in!" said Pablo, a large grin smearing his face.

"Careful what you ask for," warned Vickie as she shoved Pablo flat on the table.

"Hey! A little warning next time, eh? That way I can savor it," he said with a wink.

"Oh, I'm gonna enjoy this!" Vickie said as she examined the leg's fittings and lined the new leg up with Pablo's empty socket.

"Aight, hold him down," Vickie said.

Freya pressed down on Pablo's abdomen, and Vickie pushed the leg into the socket until it sounded a violent pop.

"Ooooowwwwwwwww!" cried Pablo. "Geesh, lady! Shouldn't we go on a few dates before you manhandle my bolts?!"

"Move your new leg," Vickie commanded.

Pablo sat up, his posture a bit woozy, and the three of them stared at the orange appendage now attached to his otherwise silver body.

"It doesn't *feel* like mine," he mumbled, watching his new foot as it rolled side-to-side.

"You're not alone. All prosthetic patients say the same thing," said Vickie.

"They do?" Pablo asked, his face brightening a smidge.

"Yes! It's natural. That orange stick poking out of your leg *ain't* your limb! But if you show up and do the work, it'll feel like it's yours soon enough. Now, have you ever ridden a bike?" Vickie asked.

"Oy!" said Pablo, his eyes wide.

While Freya watched Pablo battle synchronized pedaling, she couldn't shake the feeling that her own fans were running out of sync. Was it possible to retrain her nur-BUS system for this new environment? She felt like a clunky orange mismatched leg jutting out of the Underground. If she keeps showing up, keeps doing the work, will she feel like she belongs? Or will she always stick out, like a bright orange leg?

[12]

ARCHIE

"M...o...r...n...i...n...g... A...r...c...h...i...e," Tamika said.

"Good morning, Tamika," Archie replied, unplugging from his charging bay.

Tamika skirted out of his way. The sentients' quarters were functional but cramped, more like a closet than a living space. It was strange to Archie how so little room had been provided, given the sheer amount of underutilization within the massive residence. He reasoned humans still think of bots as mechanical, so they throw them in with the cleaning supplies.

Archie's orb pinged, indicating a message.

"Their Lordships invited me to dinner!" exclaimed Archie, his fans whirring to life as he read the words.

"W...o...w...z...a...!" said Tamika.

"You talking to that suck-u-bot?" a short robot asked, stepping out of its charging bay and nodding to Tamika.

"S...h...h...h," warned Tamika.

Archie glanced between Tamika and the stranger.

"Her? Nah. She's not much of a conversationist," said Archie with a sly smile.

The robot laughed, and Archie watched Tamika slip out the exit from the corner of his eye.

"That's a good thing... for her! You know what I mean? That little bot's seen some things," the robot said, waggling his brows.

Archie cautioned himself to stay calm and on guard. He needed to be careful not to implicate Tamika. The situation seemed more dangerous for her than he'd initially realized.

"Name's Marcus," the robot said, offering Archie his hand.

"Archie. Good to meet you," he replied.

"I've heard about you, alright. You've got Hector spinning bolts. He was gunning for your job. That listing was open for 14 weeks before you snagged it. One more week and he woulda been the one in charge right now, not you," said Marcus.

"I wouldn't intentionally take someone else's place," said Archie.

"But didn't you say you're having dinner with the Silvers tonight?" Marcus asked.

Archie tipped an eyebrow. "Yes, I've just received an invite, but I didn't ask for it."

Marcus pursed his lips. "I've never heard of sentient staff being summoned for dinner 'round here. I don't think Hector's *ever* gotten an invite. I'll have to ask."

Archie's eyes widened. "Oh my! Should I be nervous?"

"Nah. Only thing worth fussin' over is losing your gig, but if you was being fired, they'd have Mrs. R. handle it. No, I'd say it's... erm... quite an honor to be invited," replied Marcus, rubbing his chin.

"Isn't it weird to invite a bot to dinner?" asked Archie.

"Humans don't care about impositions on our kind," replied Hector.

"But what do they expect me to eat?" Archie asked.

"Maybe they'll serve a power cord with the appetizers," Hector suggested with a shrug. "So when is this thing?"

"Tonight."

Marcus winced. "Oof. That don't give us much time."

"Time for what?" asked Archie.

"Uh... to get you caught up on official dining room etiquette," replied Marcus, putting his arm around Archie's shoulder and escorting him out the door.

Archie probed the Celia's soil, smiling when the reading returned satisfactory results. All the sickly yellow leaves on the delicate violet-colored flowers had dropped and been replaced by young green buds. The size of the blooms had increased by an astonishing thirty percent.

His success wasn't limited to Lady Silver's flower garden. All the grounds had flourished, really, since his arrival. Was that why Lady Silvers had summoned him? For praise? He hoped so, but didn't want to be presumptuous. Perhaps it was Mr. Silvers who wished to see him.

"Mrs. R.'s calling for you," said a hedgebot, interrupting Archie's thoughts.

"Oh, okay," Archie replied, his brows still scrunched as he stood and brushed off the clothes he'd finally grown used to wearing.

His knees trembled as his feet ambled toward the grand house. Mrs. R had never summoned him like this before. But after Marcus's comment, he wondered if he was being fired. Could Marcus be wrong about the dinner invite being an honor?

His feet shuffled under him as he entered the residence,

his footfalls sounding with an oddly dull slap through the empty halls. He stopped, realizing he hadn't been told where to find Mrs. R. Where would she be at midday? The kitchens? Archie decided to check. At the least, there'd be bots there to point him in the right direction.

The echo of his footfalls across the pristine marble floors kept him company in the otherwise empty corridor. A squeak drew his attention to the left, but he couldn't find the sound's culprit. He paused to listen. Silence sat heavily, the way a forest goes quiet when a predator approaches. Archie, seeing no signs anyone was there, resumed course. Mere moments later, quietness vanished with a rustle as something was simultaneously thrust over his head. He groaned, struggling to grasp a sliver of the bulky cloth that'd adhered to his face, unable to gain purchase enough to tear it away.

"It's time your employment saw its end," an electronically auto-tuned voice said in a sing-song cadence.

"Shhh! Not here," said another masked voice.

"I've got his head, you grab his feet!" came the third.

The sound of duct tape ripped through the hall as Archie's wrists were bound together behind him. His feet were swept out, slamming him violently to the ground with a crash that reverberated down the halls.

"Quick, get this junker outta here," someone ordered.

Archie's legs were tied together, and his body was suspended between a pair of assailants. His processors tumbled as he was carried out. A chorus of footsteps was Archie's only clue about where he was being taken. First, they were pats against the marble that graced the majority of the mansion's main floor. Next, a breeze to tell him they'd left the mansion and were now outside. Archie knew, however, that if he were in the front yard, he'd hear the scuffing of the party traversing the pavement. Plus, the back door opens onto a brick slab patio. Hearing neither, he reasoned they must be traveling through the soft grasses of one of the side yards.

When their elevation began to climb, Archie knew they were entering the woods on the east side of the property. He pulled up his internal maps and saw there were two house-sized storage sheds and a horse stable on this side of the grounds, none of which he was familiar with. Was he being taken to one of those?

All movement abruptly stopped, and his body plunged to the ground.

"Ack! You was supposed to have the trunk open already, you dumbot! Why do I gotta do everything 'round here?!" complained one of the kidnappers.

Behind his back, Archie summoned one of his fingertip probes. Contorting his tape-cuffed hands, he maneuvered the probe to shred his way through his bindings. The screech of wrenching metal pierced the air, a triumphant announcement of the trunk popping open.

"Well?" asked the same speaker. "What are you waiting for?! Get him in there!"

Archie was shoved face-first into the trunk of a low-slung vehicle, but when his kidnappers tried to push him all the way forward, his CCO got caught on the trunk.

"He ain't gonna fit," someone said.

"I'll make him fit," promised another.

Archie was turned on his side, his body forced to contort into the space. The trunk crunched against his shoulders three times before one of the assailants suggested putting him face down. Archie's limbs were maneuvered and his face smashed into the wiry carpeting. He heard a crack as the trunk slammed into his CCO.

"Told ya he wasn't gonna fit," somebot said.

"And I *said* I'd make him fit!" said another.

"Knock it off, both y'all! Grab hold of those fans sticking outta his back. No, the black thing!" commanded the third voice, the bot Archie assumed was in control.

His body was jostled as three sets of hands each grabbed a separate side of his CCO.

"Pull!" the leader commanded.

Pain seared through Archie's body as his CCO was violently wrenched from his back.

"Shut him up! Shut him up!" somebot ordered.

"I can't!" said another, their tone panicked.

"Then get him in there, and let's bolt!"

Archie stopped being able to decipher individual voices. He couldn't hear over the screams. It wasn't until the trunk slammed shut that he realized all the shrieking was coming from him.

He returned to his senses, but his processing power was diminishing at an alarming rate. His orb glowed red, beeped a low-power warning, and blasted an alert through his system. He needed to do something, stat. He felt around, hoping to find a pull cord that would pop the trunk. But even after scooting back until he butted against the wall, he could reach very little while encumbered by bound hands.

Another alarm jolted his body, signaling that his battery was critically low. Archie's last thought before the remaining power seeped from his system and his head fell with a thunk onto the floorboard was that something was terribly amiss for his battery to drain so rapidly.

[13]

FREYA

"Oh. My. Booooolts! This is amazing!" Freya said as she lay face-down on a steel table, surrounded by mechanical arms that were buffing oil into her backside.

"Told ya you'd love the reconditioning room," Marsha grinned from the table beside her.

"No wonder you're always glowing," said Freya.

"Nothing wrong with presenting your best self. How's the new gig?" asked Marsha.

"Eh... my two-week review? Not too shabby," she answered. "I wouldn't say I'm a natural at it, but I get along well enough."

"Are you settling in otherwise?" Marsha asked.

"It's touch-and-go. I like Patchworks and my charging bay. The problem is what to do in my so-called 'free time,'" Freya answered.

"Oh," said Marsha, her eyes downtrodden. "Yeah. I remember those days. Won't lie, babes, they were dark."

"Are you happy now?" Freya asked.

"I wouldn't trade it for nothing! How are you filling your downtime now?" Marsha asked.

A smile flitted across Freya's lips.

"I go to the surface, stroll in the sunlight. Sit on park benches and watch the lil' ones play. What about you?" Freya asked.

"I'm fond of lively environments. Casinos. Nightclubs. Places like that," replied Marsha.

Freya's nose scrunched. "Sounds a bit much for me."

"But I know what *isn't* too much for you," said Marsha, donning a mischievous smile.

"Uh-oh," replied Freya.

"You're gonna love it, I promise!" said Marsha.

"Okay... what is it?" asked Freya.

"That part's a surprise," replied Marsha.

Freya bit her lip. "Oy! I hate surprises!"

"You'll love this one," Marsha promised.

Freya rolled her eyes. "You'd better be right."

"Yipee!" said Marsha.

Freya shook her head, unsure about her friend's enthusiasm. The pair of them didn't share the same tastes in much of anything.

"When is this happening?" she asked.

"I'll swing by your charging bay tomorrow afternoon at five," Marsha replied, her voice tittering with excitement.

▭

"What's this?" Vickie demanded as two guard-bots stormed into Patchworks, lugging an unresponsive robot.

"We found him stuffed inna dumpster out back. He's in bad shape," replied one of the bots, who was sporting a silver arm affixed to an otherwise orange body.

"Put him in one of the beds. And get the scissors!" Vickie commanded.

Freya scrambled to find a pair.

"Watch out for his back. Lay him on his side," said the second guard-bot, who daunted Freya with his eight-foot height.

Her brows drew close when she noticed the duct tape binding the stranger's feet. She circled the bot, who lay hunched lifelessly upon the table. His legs weren't the only things bound, she realized, as his hands also needed to be freed.

Freya stopped for a closer examination of the bot's back, a grimace painted on her face. The robot was missing its rear panel, leaving its delicate circuitry exposed. Yet at the same time, the bot's garment looked as if it'd been designed to be backless, given the stitching around the opening. But why would any bot dare to leave its components exposed like that?

Wedging her scissors into a tiny crevice, she began her cut. The bot's legs gradually loosened as she labored until he was freed. She worked on his wrists next, though it was easier because there were several punctures, giving her purchase to slice through in moments. Grabbing his knees, she pulled to straighten out his legs, but they wouldn't budge. She returned to his hands and found the same thing. Freya pursed her lips. Even a powered-down bot should still be pliable.

"I got the tape, but I can't get his legs or arms to move," Freya said.

"Machina-mortis," Vickie said somberly, as she cleaned the bot's body with a rag.

"Machine death? Are you saying that he's... is he dead then?" Freya asked, stepping back.

She'd never seen a dead robot this close before, not that they were common. They happened sometimes. But the only deaths she knew about were accidents. This didn't look like any accident, not to Freya.

"We'll find out. Could be he just ran out of power," answered Vickie.

"Or it could be they ripped the power pack right outta his back," said the guard with the mismatched limbs.

Freya's brows furrowed. "Wait... you think someone tore his back open?"

The guard nodded his head towards the gaping hole.

"You don't?" he asked.

"Well, his clothes were made to keep his back exposed," Freya said, demonstrating by running her fingers along the garment's hemmed seam.

"Lemme in," said Vickie, elbowing her way front and center.

Using a compressed-air canister, she wind-bathed his exposed circuitry. When she was finished, she polished what remained of his back plate with a soft cloth, restoring a slight sheen to his paneling that captivated Freya's attention. She longed to know the robot crouched before her. The one that looked so beautiful, even amongst death. What'd happened to him?

A rip shredded the air as Vickie tore off a piece of a milky-colored, thin cellophane wrapping and carefully pressed it onto the bot's exposed circuitry. Her fingers expertly sealed the edges water-tight. Then, using a heat gun, Vickie adhered the bandage, the wrapping hardening into an opaque shield as she did so.

"Help me break his machina-mortis," Vickie said, pointing at the two guards, who looked at each other quizzically.

Freya froze, eyes wide. What did she mean? Bring him back to life?

"If you can't help, then get outta the way!" ordered Vickie, bumping Freya on her side and causing her to roll dangerously off-balance.

Freya's mouth dropped. "Sorry, I'd—"

"Make a terrible nurse-bot," finished Vickie, shaking her head.

The bot was righted onto its backside with Vickie's guidance. Starting with his left leg, she taught them to gradually massage the appendage. The trick was getting the lubricant to flow without breaking the limb. The three worked as a team, one body part at a time, until, at long last, the robot lay flat on its back.

"Moment of truth. You want to do the honors?" Vickie asked, handing a power cable to Freya, who numbly clasped it.

The bot looked at peace, and Freya wondered if they should try to wake him. Perhaps he was better off. If he did wake, then what? It's not like his life could ever be the same. She knew what it was like to have her whole life upheaved in a day. She didn't wish that on any bot, especially this mysteriously handsome stranger. But she had to know. She had to try. Freya plugged him in.

The four bots stood in a circle around the steel bed, anxiously awaiting any sign of life but seeing none.

"Maybe he's dead," the shorter guard-bot said.

"Look! He's charging!" announced Freya, pointing to a green wisp of a pulsing line.

"Fantastic! Great work!" Vickie said, breaking out into a rare smile and patting the guards on the back.

"How long till he wakes up?" asked the looming, lanky guard.

"You mean, *if* he wakes up. I dunno," Vickie said, her smile slipping away.

Freya kept watch over the mysterious stranger as he slept, all the while resisting the urge to brush her fingers across his cheek. He hardly seemed a troublesome creature. Then again, who was she to say? Even the most troubled babes appeared angelic during slumber.

[14]

FREYA

Freya followed Marsha down a pathway too narrow for the pair of them. They rolled in comfortable silence for several minutes. She'd grown used to the long tunnels and found she quite enjoyed the scenery. It was like being in a secret world full of hidden treasures.

”You ready?” Marsha asked.

”How am I supposed to know? You won't tell me what we're doing!” Freya said.

”We're chasing a good time,” grinned Marsha.

”I'm afraid to ask what that means for you,” replied Freya.

The cave floor began to vibrate, nary a hum.

”Uh, Marsha… do you feel that?” Freya asked.

Marsha's eyes twinkled when they met Freya's.

”That's just the beginning!” she said.

The lack of alarm on her friend's face allowed Freya to settle in and let the vibrations soothe her scarred rollers. A slight breeze interrupted the stagnant air, and as the pair rounded the next bend, a grand hall opened before them.

Freya halted, mesmerized.

"What *is* this place?" she asked, wincing as her voice ricocheted off the cavern walls.

"It's the Steel Harmony Amphitheater. They run shows weekly, sometimes twice. I saw Glitch Garden here in March, and Sprocket & The Overloads in April," Marsha said.

"I had no clue robo bands were a thing," Freya said, her mouth hanging open.

"Why not?" Marsha asked with a shrug. "We need stuff to do in our free time. I ain't gonna hang 'round my charging port all day."

"Huh," Freya said, blinking blankly.

Free time was still a new concept to her, the Underground being her first real taste of it. She'd been hopping from one task to the next, one day to another, for so long that she hadn't considered it would all settle. That it'd stop. Sure, her life was now her own, but the concept remained vastly foreign.

An intimate stage where the band was setting up gear was the focal point of the room. Benches, carved of stone, circled it, with bots of all sorts scattered in seats across them. Marsha led Freya to an opening large enough for the pair of them, and they sat.

Conversation quieted to a murmur as the pluck of a bass guitar string rang through the air.

Four robots dressed in matching black-and-red tuxedos occupied the stage. Aside from the bassist, one played the violin, another the drums, and the last sat at a keyboard. The bass player rolled forward to the lone microphone.

"Gooood evening, robros! How's everyone doin' tonight?!" he asked.

Metal clanged throughout the cavern as the robots clapped.

"I'm DIM, and we're DIM and the Diagnostics!" he announced, raising his arms in the air triumphantly.

The crowd broke into a cheer. DIM smiled, then turned and nodded at the band.

"That's my robro, Alvin," he said.

The violinist raised his hand, and the cheering flared back up. Alvin began his melody.

"We've got Ricky playing keys," DIM said, as the keyboard added its voice.

"And last but not least, the bot that brings the beat, Buzz!" he said triumphantly.

Percussions stepped into the mix, and the crowd's clamor filled the chamber. The music started in earnest, and the crowd was soothed into silence. Freya swayed with the endlessly changing rhythm. For the first time in her entire existence, she thought about absolutely nothing, not even the slumbering stranger.

It was bliss.

▭

"So whatdya think?" Marsha asked as they journeyed back.

"I think... " Freya said, blinking several times, "I think it was soooo amazing that I mighta accidentally rebooted."

"Ha! I *knew* it! Now I have someone to take with me. Not that I get many evenings off," Marsha said with a wink.

"Yes, please! I can't wait to hear someone sing in there," said Freya.

"Sing?" Marsha echoed, shaking her head. "No. No one sings, babes. It's a buncha bots. Most of our voices ain't that great."

"But some do, like us nan-bots. So we can sing to the lil's," Freya reminded her.

"Ugh, I hated doing that! Human singers are much more talented. My voice is an earworm," she said, squishing her nose.

"That's too bad," pouted Freya.

"You couldn't gift me enough pretty purses to get on that stage. But *you* could try out," suggested Marsha.

Freya's eyes sprang wide and her body shuddered. Though she was talented at carrying a tune (in her own estimation, at least), the thought of singing on that stage was simultaneously terrifying.

"Eh, no thanks. How 'bout we find someone braver than me?" she replied.

[15]

FREYA

THE STRANGER still occupied the bed when Freya arrived at work that night. He showed no signs of improvement or deterioration from the night before, nor had the day shift observed any change.

"I called the guard-bots, the ones who dropped him off, for help getting him outta here," Vickie said.

"To go where?" Freya asked.

"The Pick-n-Pull," Vickie said.

Freya's mouth dropped. "We're just giving up?"

"He should've woken within thirty mins, an hour, tops. Once he had enough charge to restart his nur-BUS system. Keeping him overnight was a courtesy more than anything," Vickie said.

"But he looks so... so... *not* dead! Are you sure?" asked Freya.

"It's motherboard death," Vickie said somberly.

"But how can you be sure? You can't test for that without performing surgery," Freya said.

Vickie shrugged. "It's the only explanation."

Freya searched the stranger's face for any sign of life.

But Vickie was right. There were none. Dejected, she turned away and found herself face-to-face with Pablo.

"Whoa, robro! Where'd *you* come from?" she asked, eyes wide.

Pablo cocked an eyebrow. "The front door... where else?"

"Door sensors must be out again," grumbled Vickie.

Freya smiled jovially. "I hardly recognized you with two legs."

"Come sit," Vickie said, patting the bed next to her. " How you getting on?"

"More challenging than I'd hoped," he replied as he hopped onto the table.

"How so? Is it rubbing?" Vickie asked, grasping his new leg and stretching it while keeping a watchful eye on the joint.

Pablo scratched his head. "It's just... I dunno, hard to get my body into sync or something. I feel like I'm walking lopsided even though I'm not. And I need a battery top-off before the day is out. I never needed no power-up before."

"Aww, you need a nap!" giggled Freya.

"Your new leg is 15% heavier than your last. It's gonna take a bit to train your nur-BUS system to work more effectively. But if you keep at it, you will see your battery efficiency increase."

"So the only way to find out is with time and hard work? Sounds sus," Pablo said, crossing his arms.

"Aight, let me get a copy of your vitals, then hop on that stair stepper," Vickie said.

"For how long?" he asked.

"Till I say stop," she answered.

As Pablo grumbled his way to the cardio station, Freya rolled towards the sleeping stranger. The poor robot. He lay so still. But he looked peaceful, not dead. She ran her fingers along his gleaming chest, stopping on his orb as she wondered what the bot was like. What was his story?

She grimaced as the tips of her fingers met the remnants of adhesive mucking his face. She rummaged through a drawer, emerging with a bottle of rubbing alcohol, then methodically scrubbed at the sticky grime. As she worked her way down, her fingers probed a division between his neck and right shoulder plates that was not matched on the other side. Her brows furrowed, and she pushed the plates together, closing the fissure with a click she felt in her fingertips. Freya backed away as the bot's orb flashed red, then yellow, then faint green.

The rugged stranger opened his eyes and stared at her.

[16]

REED

THE LIGHTS... what was wrong with the lights? They were sterile, bright. Not natural. Empty beds sprawled around him. Exercise equipment was everywhere.

Where was he? How did he get here?

Movement caused his eyes to snap to attention. They widened at the creature in front of him. She was... well, she was lovely. Her steel was lustrous and well-oiled, and her features kind and nurturing. The faint blue glow of her chest orb shone against her oversized eyes, eyes that had depth, eyes that were looking right at him.

Oh crap.

Ensnared, unable to turn away, his mouth dropped. No words escaped.

"He's awake!" she shouted.

She shook her head and looked at him in disbelief. "*You're* awake. I... wow! Umm... hi! Name's Freya."

"Hi, Freya," he said, enchanted by her soft, melodical voice.

"And you are?" she asked.

That was a good question. Who was he?

"I'm... um..."

His eyes jumped to the clothing on his body, clothing that he didn't recognize. Why couldn't he remember?

"I... need..."

His eyes glazed over, and he rubbed his head. What was wrong with his memory recall?

"Your name's Reed?" Freya asked.

"Huh? No," he replied. "Well. I don't think so. Is it?"

"What else would it be?" she asked, smoothing a wrinkle from his jumpsuit.

He threw his palms up. "I don't remember."

Freya's head tilted to the side.

"What's the last thing you remember?" she asked.

"Good question," he answered, pursing his lips.

He scanned his memory banks, fighting for any scrap, a lone thread to pull on. Nothing. It was bizarre. Memory was supposed to be instantaneous, occurring without conscious thought. That's the way it's always been. Until now.

"I can't remember. There's nothing. Nothing before opening my eyes," he said with dismay.

"Before opening your eyes when?" Freya asked.

"Today! Just now!" he replied, sitting up and throwing his legs over the side of the bed.

"Wait, you don't remember *anything*?" Freya asked, her eyes wide.

"No," he said, hanging his head.

Freya pointed at his chest. "Says 'CLIMECH' right there. You come from the Salad Towers?"

"The what?" he asked.

"The Salad Towers. Are you a cloudie?" she asked.

He answered with a shake of his head.

"Would ya look at that, I had ya pegged for a goner! Name's Vickie," said the robot, offering her hand.

"I don't know my real name," he said.

"Wait, what?!" Vickie asked, her eyebrows raising in alarm.

"That or anything. Call me Reed for now, I guess," he said sullenly.

"He woke up this way," said Freya, her face falling into a frown.

"So where am I?" Reed asked, scanning the room.

"You're in the Underground," Vickie said.

Reed stared at Vickie, blinking blankly and refusing to utter the words he'd already said, words that would admit his failure to remember... well, anything. Anything at all.

"You likely wouldn't know it, even if you could remember," piped Freya.

"It's a place for freebots and refurbs," Vickie said.

The terms were foreign to him, yet he knew, instinctively, that term—no, that branding—belonged to him.

"That's me, isn't it?" Reed asked quietly.

"I'm sorry," Freya said, pain flashing through her eyes.

"Some help, please!" shouted a ballcap-wearing robot with mismatched legs who was trying to keep pace with rapidly rushing stairs.

Vickie scurried cattycorner to the machine.

"What's going on, Pablo?" she asked.

"I can't turn off this stupid dumbot!" he exclaimed.

Vickie unplugged the machine, and it crawled to a stop. Pablo climbed down and placed his hands on his knees. His ballcap tumbled to the floor, and he scrambled after it, replacing it with a huff.

"Sorry," Pablo mumbled.

Freya's eyes narrowed. "About what?"

"The hat. My scar," Pablo replied.

"I saw no such scar," Vickie said, waving her hand dismissively.

"I try to keep it hidden," Pablo said, hanging his head.

Vickie lifted Pablo's chin and stared into his eyes.

"Listen now, you ain't got nothing to be ashamed of," she said. "We all got scars running deeper than our plating, I promise you that. Covering them don't make them disappear."

"That's true," said Freya. "My feet are really scarred. No one else can tell, but it bothers me."

"And it's not like I wear these for fun, hun," Vickie said, taking off her glasses.

Freya gasped. "I've always wondered why you need those, being a bot and all."

"My ocular unit failed. I was deemed too old to repair, and so I was sent for decommissioning. But I made my way to the Underground and started a new life for myself. Got my glasses. And turns out they work pretty well. I hardly notice 'em anymore," said Vickie.

"Something's wrong with my back," Reed added quietly. "I can't see it or name it, but I know it, just the same."

"Yes! It's your rear panel. It's missing!" Freya said, her arms animated. "I thought it was weird, but your clothing seemed designed for it, so I was confused."

"Take off your jumpsuit, let's have a look," said Vickie.

Reed's eyes widened. She didn't expect him to undress here, did she?

"I... umm... is there a dressing room or something?" he asked.

"No need to be shy around us, darlin'. We've already seen all you've got to offer," Vickie said, winking.

Frowning, he unfastened the buttons of his army-green

overalls and slipped them off. And though his posture was strong and his balance steady, an ominous tingle hovered over his back.

The grimaces on the faces of those surrounding him confirmed what his instincts had already been screaming: something was wrong. Extremely wrong.

[17]

REED

THE DOOR CHIMED as an eccentric pair of robots entered
Patchworks. The first wore a long-sleeved hooded cloak. He
was dwarfed by his partner, who stood a whopping eight
feet tall.

"Whoa, boss!" said the freakishly tall robot, pointing
Reed's way. "It's him!"

Reed's eyebrows skyrocketed. Who were they? Was he
in danger? Should he run? Freya's hand patted his shoulder
in a strong, comforting motion. Her lack of alarm allowed
his nur-BUS system to calm down, and only then did he
realize his whole body had been rigid.

"About time you showed up. I called you blokes an hour
ago," complained Vickie.

"Wasn't our fault!" the cloaked robot said. "We was all
the way on the north end of campus. We need more guard-
bots! We're spread thin here."

"Am I supposed to know you guys?" Reed asked.

"I reckon not, you was mighty unconscious when we
carried you in. Name's Quentin," the stouter of the two
said, tipping his head in greeting.

"Name's Clyde," the gangly robot said.

His orb radiated a warm blue hue, making him appear friendly despite his imposing height.

"But who am I?" Reed asked, pointing to his chest.

Quentin's face puckered. "How am I supposed to know?"

"Well, why would you be carrying me about if you don't know me?" he asked.

"You was passed out inna dumpster in the east quadrant," Quentin answered.

"The can was open, and I spotted you," said Clyde.

"Fair enough," he said. "So I'm guessing you don't know how I ended up there?"

Clyde shook his head, his orb morphing to a red-tinged yellow.

"We was hoping you'd tell us," Quentin said.

"I don't remember anything," Reed said with a sigh.

"He ain't kidding none," said Vickie.

"Robro don't even remember his own name. He's calling himself Reed now," Freya said.

"For serious?" Quentin asked, squinting for a closer look at Reed.

Reed's back slumped, his resolve gone. What if there wasn't a single person who knew his identity? How can he figure out who he is with no memories?

"What's going to happen to me?" he asked quietly.

The group remained silent, their eyes collectively landing on Vickie.

"Well, I fancy you're one of us now. Welcome to the Underground," she said, a rare smile lighting up her face.

"Sweet!" said Clyde, his orb turning a bright cerulean blue.

Reed's head swiveled between the two.

"The *what?*" he asked.

"The Underground. It's a place for refurbs like us," Freya said.

"Is that what I am? A refurb?" Reed asked, examining his body, as though expecting the answer to be scrawled across his chest.

"That's what the gaping hole in your back suggests," Freya said gently.

She was right. Reed knew it somewhere, deep down. But discarded into a trash bin? What could he possibly have done to deserve that?

"Why haven't I heard about this place before? What'd you call it, The Underground?" asked Reed.

Vickie tipped a brow. "You're an amnesiac, and you're wondering why you don't know what The Underground is?"

Freya waved her hand. "Oh, come on. I didn't know what it was, and my memory works just fine. It's not like it's highly advertised."

"Well...," said Vickie, leaning in and lowering her voice, "We ain't *exactly* supposed to be here."

"Wait, what?" Freya asked.

"We don't own the land, but no one bothers us any. I don't think anyone knows we're here," answered Vickie.

"But there's *tons* of infrastructure down here! People don't build something like this and then forget about it," said Freya, slowly spinning in a circle.

"Only the entrance chamber is original. An encampment of discarded robots found the abandoned shipping container and expanded it from there," Vickie said.

"And now look at this place," said Quentin, splaying his arms. "It's an entire underground network!"

Freya rubbed her neck. "An underground network of squatters."

"Abandoned shipping containers? Underground networks? Squatters? I think I need to check my programming," Reed said, shaking his head.

"I know, right? This place still baffles me," said Freya.

Vickie snapped her fingers, then pointed to Freya.

"Since your memory's nice and fresh, how about you take him to intake, get him processed, then show him around?" Vickie asked.

Freya brightened. "I'd love to."

"That sound okay?" Vickie asked Reed.

Time alone with Freya?! The thought excited him, but he forced himself to remain collected.

"Works for me. Haven't got anywhere better to go," shrugged Reed.

Freya clapped. Reed watched the frills of her delightfully charming dress swirl about her ankles as they walked out the door together and wondered if perhaps being a refurb wasn't such a terrible thing.

[18]

REED

"Are you sure about this?" Reed asked, standing by the exit door on the eve of his maiden voyage outside of the steel wall's safety and into the tunnels.

Freya raised a brow. "I'll push the button if you want."

"I can do it," he huffed, hastily pressing it.

The steel door opened, and Freya rolled down the exit ramp. The space beyond was so dark. So dim. Unnatural.

"Umm... hello? Reed?" she asked, waving her hand in front of his face.

Reed shook his head to force himself out of his stupor and chase away the paralyzing fear that had gripped him when he saw the tunnel. An unpleasant sensation encompassed him, a force as heavy as the surrounding walls. The ones that seemed to close in on him as he forced his feet to follow Freya.

"You okay?" she asked.

"I've never been outside the encampment. Not that I remember anyway," answered Reed.

Freya's mouth plummeted.

"That's right!" she said with a grin. "You didn't get to take the slide in. That was fun."

"Is it supposed to be this... um... cramped?" he asked.

"You're in a cave, hon. It's your standard tunnel. Follow me, and I'll get you somewhere you can stretch your bolts," Freya said.

Reluctantly, Reed followed behind, distracting himself with the sway of Freya's skirt, a sway that eventually lost its rhythm to the ground's trembling. It didn't seem to alarm Freya, so he moved forward but kept silently on guard.

All his trepidation fled as the cavern opened into a grand hall carved out of stone. Reed spun with his mouth wide open, taking in the venue. There was a circular stage in the center of the room. It was adorned with fairy lights and had three female robots standing on it. Dressed in identical blue with white polka-dot dresses and bluntly cut, brunette shoulder-length wigs, they were setting up to perform.

"Are we... are robots getting ready to perform?" he asked.

"Yes!" Freya gushed as the pair took a seat in a sparsely populated quadrant of the natural stone benches encircling the stage. I saw DIM and the Diagnostics here last week!"

"Not ringing a bell," Reed said with a shrug.

"Would it, though?" Freya asked, cocking her head to the side.

"Probably not, since I didn't know robo bands were a thing," admitted Reed.

"Don't feel bad. I was clueless before my first concert here. You're in for a treat," said Freya.

"I believe it. Look at this place! *Listen* to it," Reed said, raising his voice a smidge to make it bounce. "It's a perfect acoustic echo chamber!"

"Do you listen to music?" Freya asked.

"I... I don't know. Maybe?" he said. "There's something to it, I'm not sure what."

"Oooh, maybe you used to play music for your plants!" suggested Freya.

Reed bit his lip. "Maybe... it's plausible. Studies show plants that are exposed to music are healthier and have higher crop yields. I just wish I could remember something about my life, not just random facts burned into my core memory."

"It must be lonely, living without your memories," Freya replied quietly.

Reed contemplated the statement, measuring it for truth.

"I'm more worried that when I find out who I am, I won't like me," he said.

"Why would you say that?" Freya asked, her brows crinkling.

"I think I'm from the surface," he said. "I mean, I was found fully clothed and in a dumpster."

Freya's hand flew to her hip. "Would that mean your life sucked? Cause lemme tell you something, robro—I used to be from up there. And I never felt lonely, not even once! Not until I was laid off. That's when I lost my identity. Everyone else called it freedom. I'm doing better now, but I've still got a ways to go."

"You're right, I'm sorry," Reed said, his eyes downcast.

"Being a robot is hard. And unfair. I was perfectly content with my life. Never concerned about happiness before I was freed. Never even questioned it. Didn't question anything," Freya said somberly.

"It's those humans!" said Reed fervently. "They created us. They bestowed sentience upon us. And then they threw us away! Someone ought to hold them accountable. But noooo! We're discarded, forced to fend for ourselves! Treated less than human simply 'cause we aren't. Yet they gave us consciousness. Why do that? Why curse us like that?!"

Reed's voice echoed through the amphitheater. Bots nearby glared at him.

He winced and lowered his voice. "And where do we draw the line, huh? I saw a sentient vacuum bot. A *vacuum* bot! Can you believe that?! The useful lifespan for one of those is what, three years? Then it's obsolete technology! Why make it sentient? It's a curse! A death sentence, only labeled as retirement."

Freya perked up. "Reed! Did you hear what you just said?"

"That robots deserve equality, even though we're not human?" he asked.

"No! Well, yes... but not that! You *remembered* something—a sentient vacu-bot!"

Reed's brows furrowed. "Wow, I guess I did."

He probed his memory banks for more traces, but came back frustratingly empty.

"I wish I could remember more. Like my name," he said.

"Hey, it's a start! More's gotta be on the way," Freya said with an optimistic smile.

"I hope so," he replied.

The unpleasant squeal of feedback bit through the air, and the crowd quieted. One of the band members, wearing a cowboy hat and holding a tambourine, stood at the stage's lone microphone.

"Let me ask ya'll a question," she said, strolling the stage. "Who's excited to see The Uplinks?"

The crowd erupted into a chorus of chatter.

"No, no, no!" she stomped, and the crowd stared expectantly. "I asked ya'll a question. I saaaaid, who's excited to see The Uplinks?!"

The robots began clapping. Reed joined in.

The tambourine-wielding bot cupped her hand near her ear.

"I caaaan't heaaaar you!" she taunted. "I saaaaid, is anyone here to see The Uplinks?!"

A chaotic blend of metal clanging, clapping, and cheers erupted.

"Now that's more like it! My name's Betsy, ya'll. I play cello," she said, pointing to her instrument, which sat next to an empty chair, "and this here tambourine."

Betsy jiggled the instrument at the bot beside her. "This girl right here is Poppy. She's a doll. And a super-talented violinist."

"And at the good ole fashioned piano, and yep, that *is* a certified twenty-first-century relic in perfect working order," Betsy said, walking to the bot seated at the bench and putting her hand on its shoulder, "we have Monica! And together, we're The Uplinks!"

Tender piano notes swirled about the cavern. The crowd jittered, and the atmosphere was flush with excitement.

"Let's be real for a millisec. Life as a refurb is *tough*, ya'all. Am I right?! But this robot right here," Betsy said, pointing to Reed," said something that resonated with me. Tell me, what's your name?"

Reed's eyes bulged, his internal fans whirring to max speed. Panic, sheer terror at the faces fixated on him, enveloped his processors. He force-quit some RAM, finally unlocking his ability to speak.

"Uh... Reed," he said.

Besty bit back a smile, then refocused her attention on the crowd.

"Uh, Reed here, bless his bashful bolts, is demanding Equality for robots!" she said.

Reed's mouth dropped. "Uh, that's not exac—"

"We're all refurbs down here. We know what it's like. We've experienced the shame of being deemed useless by the very people who created us!" Betsy said.

Chatter filled the amphitheater as heads around him nodded. Reed scanned the crowd. What was happening? How were his own words getting all out of control?

Betsy stomped. "That's not fair!"

Bots murmured to each other as her words sank in.

"I said," she robustly repeated, throwing her arms in the air, "that's... not... fair!"

"That's not fair!" echoed the crowd.

Betsy's tambourine fueled their cry. The audience stomped in tandem. Rumbles rattled the cavern.

A robot rushed to his feet and yelled, "Equality for robots!"

"Equality for robots!" Betsy shouted, shaking her tambourine and sending the crowd to its feet, echoing the cry.

"Now *that's* what I'm talking about! Time to get this party started," Betsy said, trading her tambourine for a seat at the cello.

Though it'd settled, the crowd made Reed nervous. He couldn't shake the feeling that things got out of control. That *his* thoughts, the words stupidly spewed from *his* mouth, had gained an energy of their own. An essence unstoppable.

"So what'd you think?" Freya asked after the concert.

"The music was amazing. The intro, not so much," replied Reed.

Freya giggled. "A bit too much attention for you?"

"Yo, Reed!" said Betsy, her voice creeping up from behind.

Reed winced, then turned to face her. "Uh... hi."

"I'm digging your whole 'Equality for robots' vibe. I think you're on to something," Betsy said.

Reed bit his lip. "Eh, I was just grumbling, I didn't mean to get everyone so worked up."

"Hey," Betsy cooed, pulling his chin with her finger to stare into his eyes. "Don't *ever* apologize for having beliefs. You hear me?"

He nodded.

"Beliefs set us apart from scrap metal. Dumbots don't have 'em. Neither does any bot in the Pick-n-Pull."

Reed shuddered.

"So what's your story?" asked Betsy. "How'd you wind up down here?"

A laugh escaped Freya's lips, and she hastily covered her mouth.

"Sorry," she said.

Betsy tipped an eyebrow.

"It's cause I was found in a dumpster and brought Underground," he said.

"He was in rough shape," added Freya.

He nodded. "And when I woke up, I couldn't remember anything. Not even my name. It's not Reed, that's all I know."

Betsy gasped. "That's terrible! What did the doctor say?"

"What doctor?" Reed asked, lips pursed.

"Dr. Perry! He's only the best doc-bot around," she replied, her head swiveling between Reed and Freya's blank stares.

"Tell ya what... I'll give him a holler, let him know about you. Is that cool?" Betsy asked.

"Sure," Reed replied with bravado, knowing he had no resources to pay a doctor but too embarrassed to admit it.

Betsy squealed. "Great! Gimmie your wrist."

Reed bared his forearm, and a beep sounded as she scanned it.

"Perfect! Keep an eye out for a meeting invite. Don't forget to check your junk mail," Betsy said, winking.

"Reed!" exclaimed Freya, grabbing him by the shoulder. "Isn't this great?! There's a doctor. Maybe he can help you!"

Numbly, Reed nodded.

[19]

FREYA

"How's THAT leg treating you, Pablo?" Freya asked.

"It's getting there. Bit slower than I'd like," he answered.

"Slow and steady wins the race," Freya chirped.

"My battery's still draining too quickly," Pablo said.

"That'll improve with these therapy sessions," said Vickie as she checked his vitals.

"So... 'bout how many more of these sessions are we thinking, exactly?" he asked.

Vickie pursed her lips. "Hmm... it'll take about six months for your synapses to resync. But your battery will never return to its previous capacity."

Pablo bit his lip. "And... erm... what if we didn't have a month?"

"What fool notion are you yacking about now?" Vickie asked.

"Well, you didn't hear this from me..." he said, glancing left and right as though he might be overheard.

"Hear what?" asked Freya, leaning in.

"We're being evicted," he said.

"What? Who?" asked Vickie.

"Us! All of us!" Pablo said, raising his arms. "The sheriff's department served the council with notice last night."

"Can they do that? Kick us out?" Vickie asked.

Freya threw a heated stare in Vickie's direction.

"What?" asked Vickie.

"I warned you about this," Freya replied.

"Technically, yes," answered Pablo.

"But why? Why would they do this?" Vickie asked, pacing the floor.

"'Cause we're squatters!" said Freya, throwing up her hands. "I saw this happen to my old downstairs neighbors, the Wheelers! Well, they were the ones doing the evicting. Same concept though. They travelled south for the winter, closed up their apartment, and left for three months. They do it every year. Turns out, a family of four scurried their way in there and holed up. The Wheelers come back, and the family refuses to leave! Can you imagine?! And it wasn't so easy to get rid of them, either. They had to hire a lawyer, serve the squatters with official notice, wait thirty days. Worked eventually, though. And that family, they trashed the inside of that place something fierce."

"We didn't take no one's homes, though," said Pablo.

"Doesn't matter, the property still isn't ours," Freya said, trying to quell her swelling panic.

She'd just gotten here. What would she do now?

"I can't believe this! I finally settle in. Finally feel like I belong. For what? Nothing, that's what!" Freya said.

Pablo kicked at the ground. "Most of the council thinks it's so they can get at the mountain's granite stores."

"Don't we mine those, though?" asked Freya.

"We do, which is why it makes sense. But me personally," he said, leaning closer and lowering his voice, "I think EFR's got 'em riled."

"EFR? What's that?" asked Freya.

"The Equality for Robots Movement," he answered.

Freya's eyes bulged.

"A movement? What?" she asked, Betsy's opening remarks flashing through her RAM.

"It's brand new and spreading quick like—even servo-bots are calling for it. The courthouse was graffitied, which got the human press involved," explained Pablo.

"How's the council going to stop us from getting kicked out?" Vickie asked.

"We can't! We don't have any legal standing. Not only are we squatters—we're bots. No one cares about us, not after they've gotten their money's worth and replace us," he answered bitterly.

Vickie rubbed her chin.

"Don't they have to give us thirty days' notice or something?" she asked.

"We're not human, so they ain't gotta do nothing, not according to the law," complained Pablo.

"There's gotta be *something* council can do, isn't there?" asked Vickie.

"We're trying to procure temporary shelter, but I can tell you there won't be space enough for everybot. But don't you worry, I'll get you two on the ark. How else will I finish my therapy?" he asked with a wink.

"Guess it's good to know people in high places," said Freya, the sickly feeling still lurking, plaguing her with doubts.

How did her life become so exhausting, and when did existing become such a burden?

[20]

REED

"Welcome, boy, welcome! Right on time, can't fault you that! Mighty fine quality, indeed! I'm Dr. Perry," a lab-coat-wearing doc-bot said, thrusting his hand into Reed's.

"Betsy told me about you. Interesting case, never heard a thing like it. Please, sit," Dr. Perry said, taking a seat at his steel desk and motioning to the empty chair on the opposite side.

"Yeah, about that," hedged Reed as he settled into his chair, "I'm not a star like Betsy. I don't have any money to pay you."

Dr. Perry chuckled. "I assure you that don't matter any, boy. We don't run on money down here," Dr. Perry said.

Reed did a double-take. "Wait, you don't? I thought that's how societies work."

"Aha!" Dr. Perry said, pointing his index finger in the air. "My dear boy, that's how *human* society works. Money is just a construct. We only need enough to purchase the few things we need. Our only expenditures are for electricity and the purchase of rare maintenance materials. We excavate only as much granite as we need to pay for these things. Labor is the thing we need most. We can't buy it. That's why it's the sole requirement for living down here."

"What if they don't want to work?" Reed asked.

"Some do choose the Pick-n-Pull path. That's their prerogative. Personally, I've never known a bot who cared to be idle. I think we're all innately driven to provide value. To work. Humans created each of us for a purpose, and we strive to fulfill it," he replied.

Reed shuddered as an image of rusted robots raced through his RAM.

"Why would any bot choose that place?" Reed asked.

"Some are tired. They're old, worn out, and unfixable. Done with life. Others fall into blackness, losing their sense of self and identity," Dr. Perry answered.

"Try having no identity at all," said Reed bitterly.

"Don't you worry, boy. I've got some theories on you," he replied.

Reed sagged back in his seat. "But if you've never seen a case like mine, how are you gonna help?"

"I've got a knack for fixing, even more than your average doc-bot. And my calling, boy, is to help others function their best," Dr. Perry said as he scanned Reed's wrist.

"Let's see here," Dr. Perry said. "Oooh, you're a cloudie!"

"A what?" asked Reed.

"A clio-bot. I'm looking at your specs now. Manufactured by CLIMECH. You worked for Spire, up in the Salad Towers. That's what we call their skyscraper farms," he answered.

Reed rubbed his neck. "That feels... erm... a bit violating. Isn't that privileged information?"

"Of course it is, lad," replied the doctor. "Being a doc-bot gives me access rights. You were hauled in from a dumpster, I hear. How long were you unconscious?"

"Nearly twenty-four hours," Reed answered.

"Precisely!" Dr. Perry said, slamming his palm on the desk. "Much longer than a bot who'd merely been drained. I suspect your CMOS—that's a battery on your motherboard that retains critical memory—became unseated, likely by the force of the climate control organ being yanked from your back."

"Wait, yanked? Why do you say that?" asked Reed.

"Stand up, boy, and turn yourself around," Dr. Perry commanded.

Reed's chair squeaked in protest as he rose to attention. The doctor's fingers probed at his back.

"Precisely as I thought. It wasn't a clean pull. The plate edging is jagged. I can see two places where your frame was broken. The world's not as safe these days," the doctor said, shaking his head. "Not like when I was tot-bot. That's what I called my infancy years."

"Learning at incomprehensible speeds and having all the world's knowledge at your fingertips didn't prevent you from blundering through life, eh?" Reed asked, smiling slyly.

"Thatta boy!" Dr. Perry said, patting Reed's shoulder. "Wisdom. It can't be bought, only earned through life's experiences."

"Why do you keep calling me boy when I'm a bot?" Reed asked.

"Habit. Left over from my first career, before becoming a refurb. I worked in human hospitals. I wasn't made to fix machines, but, like I said, I've got me a knack for fixing things," the doctor replied, his gaze distant as he fidgeted with his lab coat.

"It's not a bother. I was only curious. If my CMOS is dislodged, does that mean you can put it back in place?" asked Reed.

"Goodness, no!" said Dr. Perry, his eyebrows sky rocking. "Your CMOS is already in place. You wouldn't have woken up otherwise."

"But no one mentioned it to me," Reed replied.

"Perhaps someone caring for you inadvertently reseated it," suggested the doctor.

Reed's mind drifted back to his first wisp of consciousness, to the first face he saw. Her face. Freya's. She was there, smiling, her hands on his shoulder, when he woke. Had she saved his life?

"So if it's in place and I'm awake, what's the problem?" asked Reed.

"You don't have your memories, that's the problem!" said Dr. Perry.

"Okay. Let's say my CMOS is bad, and you go in and replace it. That'll restore my memory?" Reed asked.

Dr. Perry shook his head. "Oh no, dear boy. If your CMOS is bad, you'll never get your memories back."

"I don't get it. What's the point in replacing it then?" asked Reed.

"Because, if you ever have another total power drainage, you'll retain the memories you have now. With a bad CMOS, your memories would get wiped. Again," said Dr. Perry, looking at Reed pointedly.

Reed recoiled. "Let's fix that, please."

"Hold up. There's more. Let's say your CMOS *isn't* bad, okay? I have a theory. It came when I was watching that human movie, Frankenbot. Like they needed to do *anything* else to ostracize our kind," said Dr. Perry, rolling his eyes.

"They have no problem creating us and making us sentient. Yet they treat us all like junkers and force division between our species," complained Reed.

"Equality for robots!" said Dr. Perry, thrusting his fist in the air.

"What'd you say?" Reed asked, hopeful he'd misheard.

"Equality for robots!" repeated Dr. Perry. "Everyone's saying it. Haven't you seen the signs?"

"Signs?" Reed echoed, his RAM fuzzy and difficult to slog through.

"The ones hanging about? They're all over the amphitheater, the locker rooms, the corridors," said Dr. Perry.

"I hadn't," Reed mumbled, disoriented.

The walls seemed to press in on him. There they were again, his words. Spreading all out of his control. Growing unhinged. Accidentally birthed into the world.

"Well, it certainly sounds like you're on board with the movement," said Dr. Perry.

"The movement?" Reed asked.

Reed's fans raced to max speed. He longed to go back in time. He'd been foolish to blab so carelessly at that concert!

"What's wrong with you, boy?" asked Dr. Perry.

"Sorry," said Reed, biting his lip. "It keeps happening when I get flustered. My fans kick on, and I can't do a thing for it. Embarrasses the bolts outta me."

"Nothing to be embarrassed about, dear boy. You're sentient, just like the rest of us. Sometimes our emotions wander outside our control," said Dr. Perry.

"They do?" asked Reed.

"Why, of course! It's only natural," replied the doctor.

Being enslaved by emotion isn't natural... is it? Emotions are ridiculous, unnecessary things, and the idea of being enslaved to them is inconceivable! He's a bot for bolt's sake! He shouldn't have to deal with pesky emotions.

Yet the words struck true deep down in his core.

"I thought... I thought something was wrong with me," Reed said, still stumbling with the doctor's assessment.

Dr. Perry placed his hand on Reed's shoulder. "The only thing wrong is that you won't acknowledge them. There comes a point where you no longer get the choice to keep it in. And when that happens, they come out however they please! Outbursts, internal malfunctions, depression... it's never healthy. You asked how some voluntarily wind up in the Pick-n-Pull. Stuffing your emotions away can get you there."

The doctor stood square in front of Reed and stared him in the eye.

"Your CMOS, *that's* what's abnormal," he said. "And my theory is we might be able to jump-start yours back into submission. Kinda like shocking a human heart out of afib."

"Whoa!" Reed said, backing away. "That sounds intense."

"It does, but it's a common procedure and relatively safe," the doctor assured him.

"But it could restore my memories?" Reed asked.

"The chance of it being successful is small, mind you—13.43%," replied Dr. Perry.

"That ain't zero," said Reed, scratching his chin. "It's not high enough for me to get excited about, though. How does it work?"

"It requires an in-office procedure, and you'll have to be powered down, otherwise we might fry your operating system," explained Dr. Perry.

"Sounds... erm... tedious. Are you sure it's safe?" asked Reed.

"Most certainly!" Dr. Perry said, "The worst-case scenario is we get in there and have to replace your CMOS."

"But then my memory resets again," said Reed, his brows crumpled. "Isn't that what we're trying to avoid?"

"Ah! No no, my dear boy," said Dr. Perry. "You'd be connected to a bypass machine of sorts that'll keep current flowing through your memory core while you're powered off. That way your memory remains intact while I swap out the CMOS. Then, once it's been switched out, I'd take you off bypass and let your new CMOS take over."

"So this has all been tested? Done before?" Reed asked.

"Of course!" said Dr. Perry. "Refurbs are often geriatric. Even so-called lifetime batteries don't truly last. Not for sentients like us. This is a well-known procedure that's long been perfected."

"What happens if it doesn't work?" asked Reed.

"Nothing. You stay the same as you are now," the doc-bot replied.

"So there's no risk?" Reed asked, his brows furrowed. "I either wake up with my memories, or I stay the same?"

The doctor shrugged. "There's always a risk when the CMOS is removed that your memory is going to be reset again. But the procedure is safe and is done all the time on the aging population. And you, you're still young and healthy, with lots of service life left in ya."

Reed plopped his elbows on the desk and steepled his fingers. It sounded logical, and he needed a functioning CMOS either way. To imagine he'd been fumbling about, one tumble away from dislodging what short life he'd managed to build in this place. The thought was terrifying.

"I'm in," said Reed. "When can we set the appointment?"

"How's tomorrow?" Dr. Perry asked.

Reed gulped, his eyes wide. "Tomorrow? Um... that's good, I suppose."

[21]

REED

"Good to see you again, boy. How are you doing today?" Dr. Perry asked.

"My processors have been spinning all night. It took an extra hour to reach full charge," replied Reed.

"Relax, lad. No need to be so worried. It's an in-office procedure," soothed the doctor, standing and motioning behind him. "Shall we?"

Reed's legs rose to attention, but his RAM went fuzzy. The room seemed to close in around him.

"Right this way," Dr. Perry said, approaching the door.

It was as if his legs were made of lead, trying to get the darned things to move. He'd agreed to this, yes. But he assumed the nervousness would have fled by now. Instead, he felt sick.

Reed marched behind the doctor in silence, his emergency fans kicking on as they passed through the threshold of a narrow doorway. The room in front of him was stark, bleak. It was sterile, an operating room for bots, complete with a pedal-operated flatbed steel table and bright lights that showed dirt no mercy. The door shut, trapping him in.

He reminded himself it would be worth it as he trudged into the room.

"Go on now, have a lie down," Dr. Perry said, nodding at the table.

Reed slid onto the polished table with ease and, as he stared up, noticed pictures affixed to the ceiling. A poster full of hex code caught his attention. There was a message. What did it say, he wondered?

"I'm powering you down. You're going to get sleepy, but you'll wake back up good as new," Dr. Perry promised in a soothing voice.

"No wait, I—"

The numbers on the posters, all those ones and zeroes, faded away into a single message. Reed fought to stay awake, using the last of his open programs to stall his operating system so he could decipher the poster before his consciousness faded.

He managed to stay conscious, just long enough to read the continuous rows bearing the declaration: 'Equality for Robots!'

[22]

FREYA

CLYDE's unmistakable eight-foot-tall shadow fell across the threshold, alerting Freya to the center's visitors before Patchwork's doorbells could chime.

"Evening, Freya. Found us something bizarre here," said Quentin as he carried an unconscious vacu-bot through the threshold.

Freya raised a brow. "A broken vacuum?"

"Better!" said Quentin, leaning forward and looking around, as though afraid to be overheard. "It's a *sentient* vacu-bot!"

Freya recoiled. "What?"

"A sentient vacu-bot? Mighty waste *that* is! Sentience on something with a useful lifespan of five years tops? It's a curse, that is. Humans are cruel. Always treating us like objects. Like we don't have feelings," Vickie complained.

Freya's processors were stuck, whirring about. She'd heard about this before.

"Yo, Freya! You okay over there, chica?" asked Quentin, snapping his fingers in front of her face.

Freya blinked several times before finally having enough throughput to force her mouth to speak.

"Guys!" she said. "Reed, he had a moment where he remembered knowing a sentient vacu-bot!"

"For serious?!" asked Quentin.

Vickie's attention snapped to Quentin.

"Where'd you guys find her?" she asked.

"In the dumpster. Same place we pulled Reed. Clyde spotted her orb as we walked by," he answered.

"Uh, guys? That orb's going loco," said Clyde, pointing to its sporadic flashing lights.

"Put her on a bed, let's have a look," commanded Vickie.

Clyde carefully placed the bot on a table. Freya cleaned the circular robot, which, aside from dirt and some scratches, seemed to be in decent shape. Vickie hooked the robot to the emergency power supply, and its orb, previously a faded red, transformed into solid green. The four bots stood back and waited for the newcomer to talk, but all it did was flash.

"The voice box must've been damaged," Vickie said, picking the bot up and turning it upside down.

"Or sabotaged," said Quentin.

"Sabotage? Why would someone sabotage a bot's voice box?" asked Freya.

"To keep her from talking," Quentin answered with a shrug. "Think about it—this is the second sentient bot thrown away. Sentenced to be crushed to death, to be incinerated! It's cruel. Unthinkable. No one does that to a sentient bot, not even humans."

"What do you call the eviction notice?" asked Vickie.

"Yeah!" said Clyde. "Where the bolts are we supposed to go?!"

"Humans only throw us problems. Never the solution," scoffed Freya.

"It'll be a death sentence for a lot of bots down here. The markets will be flooded with more robots than there is work. The Pick-n-Pull is gonna have its choice of new recruits," Vickie said bitterly.

"I won't last no time aboveground. How am I going to afford power? We've never needed money down here. Don't have nothin' saved. We're not allowed bank accounts, so how could I have anything? I'm a goner!" said Quentin, throwing his mismatched limbs in the air.

"The council's staging a protest," Vickie said. "They're callin' for volunteers."

"What good's that gonna do? Do we wave our signs and expect 'em to say never mind, you can stay?" asked Quentin.

"It may be all we can do. We've gotta do *something* to get the humans' attention. Historically, it's what works for them," Vickie replied, shrugging.

"The Kelleys were activists," Freya interjected. "Protesting isn't so simple. We'd likely need a permit, at the least."

"I'm going to their informational meeting tomorrow. I'll make sure they've got their bolts in a row," Vickie promised.

Freya frowned, the weight of the eviction looming over her. She could switch industries and become Marsha's apprentice, but deep down she knew that was a path she couldn't take. A path she refused to take. Life down here was, if she dared say so, becoming enjoyable. Not just moments as fleeting as a babe's smile, but fulfillment within herself. And here it was being ripped from her feeble grasp, left to the mercy of a cruel world—a world made cruel because humans create things they don't understand. They make robots in their image, but discard them like trash. Teach them to feel, then forget they had feelings!

"I only just got settled down here, and now look at me! Back to the same spot I just crawled my way out of! If this is what freedom feels like—a day-by-day struggle to survive—then I don't want it!" Freya said, falling into a chair.

Vickie put her hand on Freya's shoulder. "We're all refurbs down here, hon. I don't know a single bot who was unhappy before becoming a refurb. It's when purpose is taken from us that we falter."

"It's easy to be happy when you're needed. Not so much when you wind up in the dumpster like her and Reed," said Freya, pointing at the vacu-bot, whose orb flashed rapidly in return.

Freya pursed her lips. "Did you know Reed?"

The robot's orb returned to a steady green state.

Freya rested her chin on her elbow. "That's so odd, cause he was thrown out just like you and—"

"Goodness, child, get with it! His name ain't Reed, remember? He don't *know* his name!" said Vickie.

The vacu-bot's orb flashed hectically.

"Oh!" exclaimed Freya, jumping to her feet. "This might help him remember. We've gotta find him!"

"Word on the street is he's got a bed in Dr. Perry's sick ward," said Quentin.

"Oh no!" said Vickie, her hand rushing to cover her mouth.

"What's that mean?" asked Freya, her eyes wide.

"It's sorta an intensive care for robots," Vickie answered.

"At least he's alive," said Clyde.

"We need to go see him. And we need to take her with us," said Freya, pointing at the vacu-bot. "She could help him remember who he is."

The little bot's orb flipped colors erratically, as though eager.

"Sure... *after* your shift," Vickie said with a wink. " Besides, she needs to charge before the journey. Unless you want to carry her."

"Get some rest, little bot," Freya said with a loving smile.

The vacu-bot's fans whirred in a melodic tone, her orb glowing pink.

Clyde chuckled, his orb beaming a friendly blue.

"Oh, don't even start, you two! We gotta get back to our own shifts," said Quentin, grabbing Clyde by his arm and pulling him away from the vacu-bot.

Freya giggled and turned to the circular bot.

"You hear that? You and I are going on an adventure first thing in the morning!" she said with a beaming smile.

[23]

FREYA

FREYA WALKED through the corridor with the robot vacuum trailing behind her. Though it was odd having a mute companion, the company was pleasant. The small bot appeared content, twirling as it traveled, undisturbed by the tunnels' seemingly endless miles of sterile steel. Functional steel. Not the pretty, polished kind humans use. Bots don't care about looks, only about function.

Her old bolts ached as they crossed over the steel box's threshold and onto the jarringly rough natural terrain. The manufactured floors were easier, more comfortable on her scarred rollers. What will she do when they're evicted? When she's forced to return to the surface? It hardly seems bearable after her Underground reprieve.

What she *really* needed to worry about was charging. Her battery's lifespan was ridiculously short. She should've taken better care of her battery when she was young. She should've followed the recommended cycles and never overcharged. How foolish she was in youth, thinking what she had would last forever!

"Whoa!" exclaimed Freya as they turned the corner.

The ceilings dripped with sparkling stalactite formations that resembled stone icicles. Pillars of glittering stalagmites jutted up, and, in several places, the two melded together into columns.

On the left, an underground river, its surface a gleaming mirror, lay largely still, save for the occasional stalactite drip.

"Did you know it takes 100-150 years for these to grow one inch?" Freya asked, pointing to a dripping stone. "The water is mineral-rich and leaves its traces behind."

The vacu-bot's orb flashed green, which Freya took as encouragement to keep talking. She risked sounding like a science teacher, but what else does one say to a sentient vacuum bot that can't carry on a conversation?

"That's why there's no steel enclosure here, to protect all of this. To think, each of these stems is so fragile that the snap of a human's fingertip could undo a hundred years of nature's hard work! Yet, given enough time, that seemingly weak rock converges into a column, overflowing and expanding over the centuries, transforming that minutely fragile thing into something that requires dynamite to blast through. It's pretty awesome to think about. You and I are mechanical, but nature—well, nature forms nature. It's an unpredictable, fascinating force," she said.

The circular bot twirled as her orb flashed green, a response Freya'd taken to mean she agreed, unlike when she flashes red and rotates her body in partial circles, like a washing machine agitating clothes.

Freya scanned the eerily still underwater lake for signs of living creatures. Expertly placed lighting bounced off the cavern walls and cast mirrored reflections upon the waters—a reflection that, while picturesque, made the task of spotting creatures cumbersome. When she could finally see the bottom, much to her disappointment, the only thing she could spy was the coated electrical line running along the bottom. The line appeared to be moving, though only slightly. Perhaps a fish had bumped it, Freya wondered.

A rumble filled the cavern. The vacu-bot's orb flashed red.

Freya pursed her lips.

"I think it's thunder," she said. "I just wish I knew for sure if we're supposed to hear it all the way down here."

The vacu-bot shuddered, its orb turning a neutral grey. Freya rolled faster, turning back to ensure her small companion kept pace.

Another rumble sounded, but this one angered the rocks. The stalactites dropped like daggers, busting upon the cavern floors with ear-piercing booms. How could thousands of years' worth of work be destroyed in mere moments, and with such deadly force?

"We've gotta get out of here!" Freya cried.

She rolled as quickly as she could, ignoring the jarring pain in her rollers. The shaking intensified, as if the very ground itself might tear apart. She clawed desperately for balance at the cave wall. She squatted down, covering her head with her arms as the ground angrily upheaved in rolling waves of destruction. A cloud of dust assaulted her oculars, which she slammed shut.

It was the longest one minute and twelve seconds of her life.

Freya waited a full minute before releasing her grip, then another before opening her eyes, which probably made no difference given the thick cloud of dust still hovering in the air. It had cleared well enough to tell that her companion was not near her feet.

"Robro? Can you hear me?" Freya called, heading back

to the place she last saw her. The path was covered in debris, and she had to keep stopping to clear rocks.

"Hello?! Little bot?" Freya called, lifting a fallen stone with a wince, fearful she'd find her companion crushed underneath. But so far, the vacu-bot was no where to be found.

"Are you okay?!" Freya called, her voice rising in intensity as she fought to quell her internal panic.

A faint pulsing red light thrust its shadows upon the wall. Its glow led Freya to her nameless friend.

How strange it was to feel bonded to someone she didn't even know. Yet they both know what it's like to be discarded. To be so-called 'free'. Free life wasn't a picnic for the vacu-bot. The poor thing, thrown into a dumpster, fated to be buried alive.

"Hang in there," cried Freya, digging her way to the corner where the light was emitting.

She hastily threw rocks behind her, stacking the larger ones up beside her, until the small bot was uncovered. Freya bit her lip at her friend's state. She was dusty, dirty, and dented. Her orb was barely glowing, and in a sporadic way, like a shorted electric signal.

Carefully, she extracted the circular bot from the rocks and carried it until the path opened wide enough for her to set it down and wipe the dust from its orb. The vacu-bot's orb flashed a reassuring green, and her fans kicked on, throwing debris out the vents as well as out her backside, where her dustbin should've been.

"You've lost your bin! I'll be right back, I'm gonna look for it," said Freya.

Her friend flashed a red warning, but Freya shrugged her off and continued the search. Walking the return path was easy. She'd already cleared it, and this time she wasn't lugging anything.

Freya located the vacu-bot's black bin near where Tamika was found, but as Freya reached for it, it jiggled out of her grasp. Her eyebrows furrowed. A rumble, the sound of tumult, poured new fear into Freya. Her balance went unsteady.

It was happening again, the world was caving in!

Flattening herself against the wall, she crouched down and covered her head. Pebbles danced on the ground, mere moments before an avalanche of stone crushed her.

Freya was oddly calm as her power faded. The world dimmed, and pure peace enveloped her. She was finally free from being free.

TAMIKA

Tamika sought refuge from the shaking world under a rock shelf. Being small had its advantages, and this time afforded her a safe place to hide. The minuscule nature of dust, however, made its avoidance impossible.

Her fans whirred at maximum speed to clear the debris. Her battery was draining quickly, but she couldn't travel until she could draw air through her system. After thirty precious minutes of draining the battery and falling to a woeful 35% power, her system gave her the all-clear to venture out.

She turned on her headlamp, but visibility was limited to a few feet. Dust hung in the air, confusing her radar and navigation and taxing her battery. She crawled at a snail's pace, scurrying around the rocks the caves had vomited everywhere while terraforming its depths. The paths were foreign, all except those she'd travelled to get there. She had taken a right turn into the cavern, she remembered that much, so she decided to search the other direction towards the place where Freya had located her.

The rocks defined her path, leaving little room to skirt

around them. She tried not to pay attention to her rapidly dropping power meter, now at 28%. Twice, she had to push pebbles out of the way with her bumper, each time costing her precious percentage points and her battery to 24%.

Carefully, she combed the wreckage, albeit with the severe disadvantage of being only four-inches tall. The path abruptly ended in an insurmountable pile of rocks, forcing her to turn around. Her low-battery alert sounded a distress signal as it dropped to 20%.

Her fans roared to life, and her battery plummeted to 17%. When her gauge dropped to 15%, her fans kicked higher. She looked all about. Would this be her final resting place? Was she destined to become a fixture of this cave? To be lost, buried, forgotten?

She willed herself to calm and preserve her power, to think clearly. Not to panic and run out of what remained of her precious battery, now reduced to 14%. She forced herself to focus on finding a solution. Since there was no longer a path going forward, she had only one choice—to preserve her precious power while returning the way she came. As she turned to go the other direction, her headlamp caught a metal glint.

Tamika veered off path to investigate, rearing back when she found Freya's arm sticking out of a pile of rocks. Following the rubble's perimeter, her short stature prevented her from seeing if Freya's face was covered, not that she could help if it was. Now 12%, she was out of time to find her way back. At least she'd located Freya. Maybe she could get someone to follow her if she flashed her orb at them enough.

Life was frustratingly lonely for Tamika, living in a world where humans assume she's dumb and robots don't know what to do with her. And when she finally finds someone who can converse with her, he goes and gets himself kidnapped!

It was all her owner's fault. She's heard the whispers, the people calling her a freak. Saying she shouldn't be sentient. As if she were given a choice. Like any bot was given that choice!

It didn't help that she wasn't able to keep a conversation with anyone, not since her owner died. Mr. Trilling found conversing in Morse code exciting and called it secret messaging. He wanted a spy bot, something mistaken for an ordinary dumbot, though his life never warranted anything worth keeping hidden. The people who carried her away called her owner a 'kook,' whatever that meant. And though he'd always have a special place in her heart, his affinity for welding together old and new technologies resulted in many interesting experiments, and was the way she came into existence.

She never noticed the differences between her and the other bots while Mr. Trilling was alive. She hadn't been lonely then, either. But life as a freebot had her wandering through a world she didn't fit into. A world where people question her right to belong, her right to exist, as though she'd asked to be created. She'd forgotten what it was like to talk to someone, to be understood, to have a conversation. That social interaction piece was missing, and she hadn't known how vital it'd been until it was snatched away.

Tamika needed to find Archie and get him restored to the Silvers' household. It'd been so long since she'd last spoken with anyone. She'd contented herself the best she could, but now that she'd had a taste of what was missing, the thought of going back to a lonely world without a single person to understand her was unbearable. She'd almost rather go to the Pick-n-Pull, but they probably wouldn't want her.

The sensors on her bumpers saved her from running into the steel entry door. Relief rushed her RAM. Inside would be far kinder to the 10% of her battery that remained. It was when she reached the door that she realized her fatal logic error: the door was closed. She hadn't thought about needing to open it all by herself.

Tamika backed far enough away to see the entire door and the control panel, which was entirely out of reach. She'd made it all that way back, and for nothing. Her orb emitted a distress signal, sending red light pulsing off the cavern walls.

What was she going to do? What could she do? It's not like she can reach the handle or the panel. It'd done no good for her to make it all this way, only to fail here.

She wondered how long the remaining 7% battery would last in standby mode. It might be prudent to shut down, but then she risked missing any good Samaritans that passed while she was sleeping. She'd have to wake in short intervals, but would that be better or worse on her remaining battery?

The steel door creaked open, startling Tamika but filling her with hope.

A robot in a white lab coat stepped out and allowed the door to close softly behind him. His gaze targeted Tamika.

"Why, a sentient bot that speaks in Morse code! And here I thought I'd seen about everything," he said, kneeling in front of her.

Tamika jolted. He'd understood her!

"I saw your S.O.S. What's wrong, little one?" he asked.

"C...a...v...e... t...u...n...n...e...l... c...o...l...l...a...p...s...e," she spelled.

"Oh my! Is someone hurt? Did you have a companion?" he asked.

"Y...e...s... n...e...e...d... h...e...l...p," she answered.

"Can you show me the way?" he asked.

Tamika's orb flashed green, and she raced for the pile of boulders that'd claimed her friend.

"How many are there?" the doc-bot asked.

"O...n...e," responded Tamika.

The doc-bot cleared the rocks out of their path as they traveled.

"There's not much out this way," he said. "Where were you guys headed?"

"D...o...c...t...o...r... P—"

"Doctor Perry? You were going to see Doctor Perry?" he asked.

"Y...e...s," she answered.

The robot grinned. "That makes sense, 'cause my office and sick ward are about the only things back here."

Tamika halted and eyed her rescuer. Was it his office? Was he the one she'd been looking for?

"R... u... D...o—"

"Yes, I am! Dr. Perry, the one and only. Pleased to make your acquaintance," he said with a bow. "But why visit me?"

"F...r...i...e...n...d...   i...n...   w...a...r...d," Tamika responded.

"Oh! You know Reed?" the doctor asked.

"N...o," she said, her orb flashing red.

"But he's the only one checked in right now. Are you looking for someone who's already been released?" he asked.

"A...r...c...h...i...e," spelled Tamika.

The doctor scratched his head. "Archie? I don't recognize that—"

He snapped his fingers.

"Archie! Is that Reed's real name?" he asked excitedly.

"Y...e...s," she answered.

Dr. Perry clapped. "Isn't that swell?! I can't wait to tell him! Unfortunately, he's unconscious right now."

"W...h...y?" she asked.

"He underwent a procedure to get his memories back, but there was a problem during the surgery. I'm hoping he wakes, but can't promise he will," replied Dr. Perry, shaking his head.

Tamika and Dr. Perry stopped in front of the large pile of stones that had originally forced her to go back the way she came.

"Well, this is problematic, given my office resides this way," he said.

Tamika turned around, following the perimeter and tracing it until she found her friend's hand. She signaled an S.O.S., and Dr. Perry rushed over.

"Oh my," he said.

The doctor carefully removed a single rock at a time until Freya's entire body was uncovered.

"C...a...n... u... h...e...l...p... h...e...r...?" she asked.

Dr. Perry brushed the rubble from Freya's face.

"Too early to tell," he replied. "Her bottom half is completely crushed, but her motherboard might still be intact. Regardless, she'll need transplants to walk again."

Tamika shuddered.

"I promise I'll do everything I can to help her," he said.

Her orb lit blue, the color of a cloudless sky. The color of hope.

"Look what I found," the doc said, reaching over Freya and flashing a black dust bin. "This must be yours."

"Y...a...y...!" she said.

"May I?" asked the doctor.

"Y...e...s," she answered.

Dr. Perry gently snapped her bin into place. It was good to be whole again—and a *lot* less drafty. But, for some odd reason, the room around her was dimming. She had a nagging suspicion that something was wrong, but her processors were fuzzy.

Her system bleeped an alert tone, and she realized her battery was critically low.

"B...a...t...t...e...r...y," she warned as darkness swallowed her.

[25]

TAMIKA

Hadn't it been dark a few moments ago? Yet it was brighter than the daylight streaming through the Silvers' floor-to-ceiling windows. And where did those windows go? Instead, monitoring equipment was abundantly splayed across the walls. She appeared to be in a room of steel tables, precariously perched on top of one. Everything around her gleamed. Even the walls shone.

Tamika performed a 360-degree scan of the room, creating a rough map. The left side led to an empty corridor. The other was lined with steel tables, five on each wall, with the foot of each bed facing the foot of the bed on the wall opposite. Two beds were occupied, but she couldn't see their faces because her vantage point was too low. But she recognized Freya's arm. She must be in the hospital, she realized.

"My, you were quick to wake, little one," said Dr. Perry, startling Tamika as he rounded the corner.

"T...a...m...i...k...a," she spelled.

"Tah-mee-kah. Tamika? That's your name?" he asked.

"Y...e...s," she said.

"Pleasure to meet you," he said, and pulled out a canister. "I come bearing combustible air to clean out your internal components. May I?"

"P...l...e...a...s...e," she answered.

The doctor smiled. "Wonderful."

The crisp air was a welcome intrusion to her clogged system, providing blissful relief with every hiss. The doctor worked methodically, not letting up until air flowed unhindered through her system.

When he was finished, she kicked on her fans and twirled in delight. Her motor purred like it hadn't since... well, since her owner died.

Dr. Perry chuckled and grabbed a soft rag.

"May I?" he asked.

Tamika responded affirmatively, and the doctor gently wiped her body clean.

"T...h...a...n...k... y...o...u," she said.

"My pleasure, little one," said Dr. Perry, leaning to examine Tamika's front bumper. "Your name was etched here the whole time, wasn't it?"

She twirled, her orb pulsing green.

"F...r...e...y...a?" she asked.

"Ah, is that your companion's name? Quite lovely indeed. How do you know her?" he asked.

"P...a...t...c...h...w...o...r...k...s," she answered.

"How do you know Re—I mean Archie?" asked Dr. Perry.

"S...u...r...f...a...c...e... c...o...w...o...r...k...e...r...s... f...o...r... S...i...l...v...e...r...s," she replied.

"You two work together on the surface?" he asked.

"Y...e...s," she answered.

"For the Silvers? As in, *Governor* Silvers?" he asked.

"Y...e...s," she answered. "K...i...d...n...a...p...p...e...d... a... t... w...o...r...k."

"So he was indeed kidnapped," said Dr. Perry, rubbing his chin. "That was my theory for how he got into the dumpster."

"I... w...i...t...n...e...s...s...,... g...e...t... c...a...u...g...h...t," she said.

His eyebrows shot up. "Are you that second kidnapping victim I just heard about?"

"Y...e...s," she answered.

"Whatever in the world is going on up there?!" he asked.

"S...e...c...r...e...t... p...l...o...t," she said.

The doctor stepped back. "Whoa! Hold up... is the governor doing something shady?"

"N...o...,... a... b...o...t," she replied.

"A robot is scheming? That's even worse," Dr. Perry said.

"3... b...o...t...s...!... H...e...c...t...o...r...,... A...l...e...j...a...n...d...r...o...,... a...n...d... M...a...r...c...u...s," she said.

"Okay, three bots, got it. Do they all work for the Silvers?" he asked.

"Y...e...s," she answered.

"And what do they want?" he asked.

"U...n...d...e...r...g...r...o...u...n...d," she replied.

His eyes bulged. "What?"

"G...r...a...n...i...t...e," she said.

"They want the granite? But why? Robots can't profit from it, not when we can't own a bank account or assets. What's the benefit?" asked Dr. Perry.

"S...T...A...N...D," she said, shimmying her body in an excited fashion.

Dr. Perry raised his brows. "The company that's bidding for the Underground?"

"H...e...c...t...o...r...s... c...o...r...p...o...r...a...t...i...o...n," she answered.

"Funds can be held in a corporation, sure, but he can't legally own one. It's illegal. The thought's absurd," decided the doctor, shaking his head. "He'd never be able to get the necessary paperwork."

"G...o...v...e...r...n...o...r," she replied, flaring her fans.

His jaw dropped. "That's... wow. That's right. He's connected, straight up to the highest power in our state. The wrong person—or bot—could get away with a lot working in his household. But, wow... bots scheming the system? Bots *scheming*? Scheming bots disgust me. They're a blight to our kind."

"A...g...r...e...e," she replied.

"Oh. My. Goodness," said Dr. Perry, freezing in place. " Are you saying the eviction notice is *their* doing? Those... those scheming freebots?!"

"Y...e...s," she answered.

He smacked his head. "Unbelievable! Now those schemebots are going to cause all of the Underground to become homeless! Have they no integrity?!"

"S...c...u...m...b...o...t...s," replied Tamika, with a shudder.

"I rarely use that degrading term, but you're right. They're scumbots. Pure scut," he said, crossing his arms.

"M...u...s...t... t...e...l...l... S...i...l...v...e...r...s," she said.

"How? I'll never gain an audience with the governor," he replied.

"A...r...c...h...i...e...?" she asked.

"He's gotta wake up first. And if he still doesn't

remember who he is, well then it might be hard to convince him to help," he said.

"T...r...y," she replied.

A cheerful chime cascaded out of her speakers. Her charging was complete.

"D...o...w...n," she said.

His brows furrowed. "Already? Tamika, my dear, I think you should rest."

"C...h...a...r...g...e...d," said Tamika, bored to death at the thought of being confined to a steel table.

"Fine," Dr. Perry said, placing her gently on the ground. "You can help me keep an eye on Archie and Freya. Hopefully one of them wakes soon."

[26]

REED?

Fluorescent lights probed at his eyelids till they retracted. Something was terribly wrong... everything was fuzzy. Shouldn't he be able to see? He spent several minutes refining his ocular's resolution, until cones became light fixtures and rectangles became beds.

Wait, beds?

He sprang up far too rapidly and was forced to re-focus his oculars. A power cord lay draped over his arm, plugged into the wall. Another connected him to a computer monitor that was displaying his vitals. Steel tables lined the room's perimeter, all with similar setups. All were empty save for his and one other, which held an unconscious bot. The room was perfunctory, clearly a hospital ward, with gleaming floors. But why was he here?

Background noise, perhaps a mechanical whine of sorts, pecked at his processors till he paused to ponder. It almost sounded like humming. What was it? He looked all around but couldn't find a source. Where was it coming from? It kept getting louder, so it must be headed his way. He raised an eyebrow, but staved off alarm. There was something familiar, almost melodic, to the sound. The volume ballooned until, at last, a small orb-bearing circular bot rounded the corner.

A sentient vacuum bot? He reared back. Why would there be such a thing?!

The little bot spotted him and spun in place, her orb green and blinking. There was something familiar about her, but he couldn't grasp what. He zoomed in his oculars, but she turned and fled before he could sharpen their focus.

The world spun, forcing him to lie flat and wonder who that bot was, why he'd ended up down here, and where 'here' was. He needed answers. He knew he was in a hospital. So obviously, something was wrong with him. Could he be paralyzed, unable to move? He stared at his foot, willing it to wiggle, and sighed in relief as it obeyed.

He swung his legs over the side of the bed, yanked the monitoring cables from his body, and swayed woozily, his processors protesting. The shiny steel floor just underfoot seemed both close and impossibly far.

The impending hum of the vacu-bot distracted him. This time, it was accompanied by pounding footsteps. A friendly-looking, lab coat-wearing doc-bot turned the corner, appearing with the hoover vac on his heels. This bot was familiar, though he couldn't fathom why. He reasoned it was possible he'd met him somewhere.

"Aye, lass! Good to see you sitting up!" the doc said, patting him on the shoulder. "How're you feeling?"

"Confused," he answered bluntly.

"Understandable. Let's start simple. Can you tell me your name?" he asked.

He bit his lip. The doctor wanted to know his name. That should be at the tip of his memory recall. Instead, it was fuzzy, something he had to grasp for and pull from the weeds of his mind.

"It's... it's... Reed, right?" he answered.

A frown flashed across the doctor's face.

"That's right, boy. That's right," answered the doc-bot.

The vacu-bot's orb flashed erratically.

"Not yet," the doctor said to her, shaking his head.

Reed's eyes narrowed. Were those coded messages coming from that bot's orb? Was there a pattern to them?

"What about my name, do you remember it?" asked the doctor.

Reed's brows rose. "Should I?"

"Hmm," the doctor said, frowning. "You should remember me, even if my name escapes you."

"You look familiar. So does she," Reed said, nodding his chin towards the vacu-bot.

"This is Miss Tamika. She's my little helper," he said fondly.

"What *is* this place?" Reed asked.

"A hospital, of sorts. Most people just call it Dr. Perry's sick ward," he replied.

"Am I sick?" asked Reed.

Dr. Perry hesitated. "Not sick... recovering."

"From what?" Reed asked.

"Heh," replied Dr. Perry. "As irony would have it, a procedure to restore your memories."

Reed cocked his head. "What's wrong with my memory?"

"How 'bout you tell me the last thing you remember?" asked Dr. Perry.

"I... I don't. I don't remember anything," he replied. "I don't know you, I don't know your assistant. Outside of you two looking familiar, I've got nothing."

Memory hadn't been something he'd had to think about before. It'd always just been there at his recall. Any memory delays were the fault of his nur-BUS system or his RAM. Never anything like this.

"This wasn't one of the anticipated outcomes," the doctor said, rubbing his neck.

"Anticipated outcomes of *what*?" asked Reed.

"Of the procedure you underwent to replace your CMOS battery," the doctor answered.

"Is that procedure why I can't access my memory?" Reed asked.

Dr. Perry opened his mouth, hesitated for several moments, then shut it.

"I'm not precisely sure. There was a slight problem during the surgery," he finally answered.

Reed's eyes went wide. "You're scaring me, doc."

"To replace your CMOS, we had to temporarily remove it and put you on bypass. Now that's a highly reliable standard procedure, mind you. But for some reason, the system hiccupped while you were hooked to it."

"Hiccupped? How does a life support machine hiccup?" Reed asked, his voice rising an octave.

Dr. Perry shrugged. "That's the best way to describe it. A brownout caused the power feeding the system to fluctuate. I sent the system for diagnostics, but haven't gotten the results back yet."

"What does that mean for me?" asked Reed.

"I wish I knew. The event was brief, and power never fully ceased. There's a chance your memories were retained. But it's also possible you permanently lost them during the flux."

The vacu-bot's orb flashed.

"That's true," Dr. Perry said to Tamika before turning

back Reed's way. "You remembered the name Reed, so you have some of your memory. Perhaps all you need is a little time for the rest to return."

"How much time?" Reed asked.

"Impossible to tell. It could be a few days or a month. Or you might never remember anything besides your name," Dr. Perry replied, sympathy twinkling in his eyes.

"When will we know?" Reed asked.

"We might already have our answer, but I pray not. If we're lucky, your memories are only delayed because they're being re-indexed. In that case, they'd naturally be restored over time," answered Dr. Perry.

"Okay... how long would that take?" Reed asked.

Dr. Perry bit his lower lip. "Hard to say, but I should think within 24 hours. 72, tops."

Reed pursed his lips. "You guys seem mighty familiar, so hopefully that's what's going on."

The vacu-bot twirled, her orb flashing.

"Both of us?" asked the doctor, steepling his fingers. " That's interesting. You see, Tamika knows you from before you lost your memories the first time," Dr. Perry said.

"I don't even know how to wrap my processors around having lost my memories twice," said Reed, shaking his head. "What if it never stops? What if my memory keeps resetting? You'll have to rename me short-circuit!"

"Ha!" said Dr. Perry, patting him on the back. "Good cheer and a sense of humor always bodes well for recovery statistics."

"You've now remembered things from before and after the kidnapping. That's promising," the doctor said.

The doctor's attention turned to Tamika, whose orb was blinking.

"Tamika says you're a refurb who works for the Silvers," said Dr. Perry.

"Silvers? That doesn't ring a bell," replied Reed.

"It's an extremely influential family. Home to the governor of our state. You're the groundskeeper," said the doctor.

Reed brightened. "That sounds like a fun gig."

"She also said that you were, erm, kidnapped by someone named Hector," said Dr. Perry.

Tamika spun, her fans roaring to life.

"Apologies," said Dr. Perry. "You were kidnapped by three individuals: Hector, Marcus, and Alejandro. Do any of those names sound familiar?"

He did a double-take. "What?! Governor's mansions? Kidnapping? This all sounds absurd. And for what, a gardening job?"

"Give yourself some credit, lad. You're a clio-bot, precisely designed to tend any plant with perfection," said Dr. Perry.

"A clio-bot? I thought I was a refurb," Reed said.

"You're both," replied Dr. Perry. "Or rather, you *were* a clio-bot, and now you're a refurb. One who lives underground—though that seemed to be Hector's will, not your own."

"We're beneath the ground?" asked Reed.

"Yes, in a vast underground cave system," answered Dr. Perry.

Reed tapped the wall beside him. "And the steel?"

"It's our encampment. Climate control. We wouldn't survive down here long without it. The humidity wreaks havoc on our systems," answered the doc-bot.

"And I live here? Not with the Silvers?" Reed asked.

"You've got a space in the locker rooms. We didn't know

who you worked for before Tamika here showed up," said Dr. Perry.

"What's up with that, anyway? How are you guys communicating?" asked Reed, his gaze split between the two.

"Ah, yes!" the doctor said. "It's the most fascinating thing. She speaks in Morse code."

"Clever," said Reed.

"Agreed," replied Dr. Perry.

"What was I doing before she showed up? Before the procedure?" asked Reed.

"You haven't been assigned a position yet. You've been in rough shape since the start. The kidnappers tore off your CCO, and with it unseated your CMOS. You were brought in unconscious," Dr. Perry said.

Reed shook his head. "My CCO? What's that?"

"Your climate control organ. According to your schematics, it was externally housed on your back. I fixed you up the best I could. You'll like the improvements. For one, you're the proud new owner of a shiny new back plate!" Dr. Perry said, patting Reed mid-back. "I was able to modify some of the connections to the CCO's sensors and internalize some of its functions. Unfortunately, you'll only be able to find another CCO through the Pick-n-Pull, and that'll be subject to organ donation laws. The other option is to fit you with aftermarket equipment, except there is none for you."

Tamika's orb flashed, and Reed admonished himself to pay attention next time.

"I'm inclined to agree with Tamika," Dr. Perry said.

Reed tipped an eyebrow. "Sorry, I wasn't paying att—"

"She wants to take you to Lady Silvers. Hector

kidnapped her, too, and she's been here since, looking after you," said Dr. Perry.

Her orb flittered red.

Reed's palms flew up. "Whoa, wait a millisecond! It doesn't sound safe for either one of us to go back there!"

"You'll have protection, of course. I daresay that's prudent," added Dr. Perry.

"They've gotta be warned about Hector. His corporation, STAND, is bidding for the underground," answered Dr. Perry.

"Erm, none of this sounds appealing to me," replied Reed. "Can't I just stay here?"

"You could, but then you'll have nowhere to go when we all get kicked out in three days," replied Dr. Perry, splaying his palms.

"Kicked outta where?" asked Reed.

"Here, the Underground, our home! We're being evicted," Dr. Perry lamented, his head hanging.

"I don't understand," Reed said.

"None of us do, dear boy," the doc-bot said, waving his hand. "Everyone's been reeling since getting the notice."

"I don't remember the Silvers, so I don't see what good it'll do me to go," protested Reed.

"You'll be remembered by someone in the household, regardless, even if they're simply staff," answered the doc-bot. "Besides, Tamika has enough intel to bring that greedy schemebot Hector down. If both of you show up together, you'll be unstoppable. They'll *have* to listen."

"I dunno... thinking about going up to a stranger makes my RAM rattle," said Reed, wondering whether they would feel familiar to him the way Tamika and Dr. Perry did.

"You'll be glad you did when you have somewhere to

live after the eviction," said Dr. Perry, staring at Reed pointedly.

'S...O...S," pleaded Tamika in a pulsing red message.

Reed smiled bravely, but the truth was, he was intimidated by the amount of happiness radiating from that pint-sized sentient bot. And terrified that he'd find his real life, the one he can't remember, to be entirely dissatisfying and lacking in simple joy.

He wouldn't know unless he tried, so Reed pulled his shoulders straight and his chin up.

"When would we leave?" he asked, striving to keep the trepidation he felt from lacing his voice.

"Tomorrow," Dr. Perry answered enthusiastically. "I'll procure backup and make sure your systems are primed. Let's check your logs. Hop up for me."

Reed planted his feet on the ground, and, though he rose carefully, still wobbled to maintain his balance. As his vision cleared, his new vantage point allowed him a glimpse of the face in the bed across from his.

"That's Freya!" Reed said, rushing to her side, his unsteadiness gone. "What happened to her?"

Dr. Perry sighed. "Ah, yes. She was, unfortunately, involved in a cave collapse."

"How is she? Will she be alright?" Reed asked, brushing his hand across her cheek.

The doctor patted Freya's legs. "Her legs were crushed, poor dear. But I was able to replace her trunk. So if she wakes, she will feel marvelous, better than new."

"Whoa, whatdya mean *if* she wakes?!" Reed asked.

"Anytime someone has a transplant, there's a chance it'll be rejected by their nur-BUS system. If that happens, she won't come back online. Her lights will be on, but no one will be home," explained Dr. Perry.

"Nur-BUS death," Reed said solemnly.

Freya looked so peaceful lying there. Beautiful, too. Shiny, well-oiled, her new legs gleaming. But if she didn't wake, she'd be the prettiest bot in the Pick-n-Pull.

Reed's fans spiked at the sudden mental image, and an intense draft caused him to squeal.

"Relax, lad. I installed two new internal fans while I was working on you. Your core temperature readings had me concerned," the doctor said.

"Oh," said Reed as he slowly counted bytes, forcing his new fans to simmer.

"Do you realize you remembered her name?" the doctor asked softly.

Reed blinked blankly. He'd pictured her face as he awoke on that cold steel table as though it'd been seared into his hard drive.

"No, I didn't," he said after a several-millisecond pause, "but I think I met her after I lost my memory," he said.

Dr. Perry grinned. "Fabulous! You're correct, lad. Fantastic progress, indeed. I've got full confidence your post-amnesia memories are still there, and I'm hopeful the rest are too. All signs suggest your missing memories are lurking, waiting for your nur-BUS system to reactivate their pathways."

"Then let's do it," said Reed, placing one hand on Freya's shoulder and fixing a determined gaze on the doctor. "Freya saved my life. Her hands reseated my CMOS. The Underground is her home, so I owe it to her to try my best to help. I'll go."

[27]

REED

THE ELEVATOR DOOR DINGED OPEN, and a group of misfit robots exited, Quentin at the helm. The hall reverberated with the hum of Tamika's vacuum and the clattering of Clyde's humongous feet. Reed and Quentin walked more judiciously, but trekking on stainless steel was seldom silent. Sunlight smacked Reed as Clyde pushed open the door to the Underground's chambers.

Reed shaded his oculars with his hand, unprepared for the shockingly bright light. He hadn't been lacking for light in the caverns, but it didn't have the same feel to it, the same livelihood. This was the warm embodiment of life and a substance he'd somehow managed to miss, even absent any memory of it.

Quentin's jaw dropped. "What the—"

Reed followed Quentin's line of sight to a pair of mustard-yellow bulldozers positioned near the cave's entrance. Signs painted with phrases such as 'Robots Rights Matter!' jutted from the surrounding rocks, but it was the ones painted with 'EFR' that beckoned his attention.

Reed halted.

"Equality for robots," he said. "That's what EFR stands for, right?"

"You got it, buddy!" said Quentin, patting Reed's back enthusiastically.

"Is that from before or after my amnesia?" Reed asked.

"Uh, after," replied Quentin, rubbing his chin. "Yes, after."

"Guys, Tamika's trying to tell us something," interrupted Clyde, pointing at the jittering bot.

"S...T...A...N...D," spelled Tamika.

"I don't understand," said Reed.

"B...u...l...l...d...o...z...e...r," she said.

Reed's eyes locked onto the signage gracing each bulldozer driver's side door.

"STAND, LLC. Strategic Terrain & Natural Development," he read aloud.

"H...e...c...t...o...r...'...s... c...o...m...p...a...n...y," Tamika said.

"What a scumbot! I'd like to get a hold of him," said Clyde, pumping his fist into his opposite palm.

Tamika forged the way ahead, whirling as she went.

━

"This place always gives me the creeps," Quentin said, trying to peer over the bleak gray concrete wall with the letters 'EFR' spray-painted on it.

Clyde hoisted Quentin by the shoulders, lifting him three feet off the ground.

"Hey! Hey!" yelled Quentin. "I hate when you do that!"

"Helping you see, is all," said Clyde.

"Well, you can put me down now," grumbled Quentin.

"W...h...a...t... d...o... u... s...e...e...?" Tamika asked.

"It's the Pick-n-Pull," answered Quentin.

Reed's eyes raked the rows of rusted, dilapidated robots. Many were missing parts, parts that'd been scavenged for refurbs. Except now, refurbs weren't an abstract concept. They were bots he knew. Bots like him, now made piecemeal. And like Quentin and Pablo, who lived with mismatched limbs. All of them, picking up the fragments of broken lives and redefining themselves at the toll of those who failed to persevere.

Tamika shuddered, her orb a foreboding blood red.

"It's a graveyard," said Clyde, grimacing.

"Heh," said Quentin. "A graveyard for the permanently retired. Those who can't afford to stay powered up."

Tamika's orb flickered impatiently from the sidewalk.

"Which will be us if we don't keep on our way," warned Reed.

Tamika zoomed off, and the others scrambled to follow. Sparse construction gave way to new buildings and corner shops as they travelled along. No one paid the group much attention, save for the occasional double glance directed at the sentient vacuum bot. As the group neared the heart of the city, the streets became cluttered, and it was decided— much to Tamika's dismay—that Clyde would carry her until the crowds thinned.

Reed squinted at the sign arched over the intersection. The Salad Market sat at the epicenter of city chaos. Humans and bots alike rummaged through an entire city block of wooden stands, all clamoring to pick perfect produce and barter the bill. Reed's sensors picked up readings simply from the abundance of plants. The atmosphere felt like being back on the grow floors, he thought.

His head jerked.

"I remember working the grow floors!" he announced excitedly.

"L...o...o...k... u...p," said Tamika.

He spotted a pair of 45-story towers, each wrapped in floor-to-ceiling windows.

"That's Spire Farms!" he said, his jaw dropping.

Tamika's orb glowed green.

"That's where you used to work, right?" Quentin asked.

"I... I think so?" mumbled Reed.

He halted in front of a Spireberry stand, his sight fixated on the bundles of beautiful blush-colored berries. Crates full of plants, the same plants he used to cultivate, were laid out for sale. Reed's vision darkened, and his fans spun, uninvoked. Memories of Spire Farms overwhelmed him—including the devastating misdiagnosis that cost him his career.

Reed's shoulders hunched, and Clyde's hand landed on his back.

"What's wrong?" Clyde asked.

"Nothing," Reed said, shaking his head. "It's my memories, they're coming back. I remember working in the towers now."

Tamika halted in front of Reed's feet, fans whirring.

"N...a...m...e...?," she asked.

"Mine?" he asked, raising his eyebrows. It's Reed."

"N...o," she said, with a half-spin.

Reed started.

"My name's *not* Reed?" he asked.

His processors paused, saturated by the sudden news. The world warped, as if time itself stuttered.

"A...r...c...h...i...e," she said.

His mouth fell open.

"Archie," he repeated as the name swirled through his processors.

Tamika's orb emitted a pulsing, multicolored light, reminiscent of a disco ball.

"H...i... A...r...c...h...i...e...!" she said, her orb glowing blue as she spun in place.

"Aww, it's an Archie!" said Clyde, his orb matching her hue, and landing a celebratory smack on the clio-bot's back.

"Why didn't you tell me sooner?" Archie asked.

"D...o...c... s...a...i...d... w...a...i...t," she answered.

His brows furrowed. "Then why tell me now?"

"A...l...m...o...s...t... t...h...e...r...e," she answered, turning to race down the street.

The group scrambled to follow, soon stopping in front of an ornate gate taller than Clyde. The name SILVERS, written in elegant script and welded from antique bronze, overlaid its top. Brick pillars encased the sides, a callbox and speaker built into the left.

"Who do I ask to see?" Archie asked.

"M...r...s... R," Tamika spelled.

Archie pursed his lips.

"Hmm... it sounds familiar... I think," he said, pressing the gate's call button.

"Identity and purpose," a curt voice cut through the gate's speaker.

"Name's Re—Archie, here to see Mrs. R," he answered.

"Identify your companions," the voice replied.

"This is Tamika. She works here," Archie said, picking her up and waving her in front of the camera.

"H...e...y...!" she complained.

"Sorry," he said, setting her back down. "They can't see you down there."

Archie pointed to the taller of the two guard-bots.

"Giganto over here is Clyde. He's a friendly giant," he said.

Clyde smiled, his orb emitting a warm blue. Archie nodded to the other guard-bot.

"And that's Quentin. They're our escorts," Archie said.

The box buzzed beside Archie, startling him.

"East entrance," commanded the bot-in-the-box.

Archie looked at his companions, and a smile spread across his face.

"Let's do this," he said.

ARCHIE

"Is there a house 'round here somewhere?" Quentin asked, shielding his eyes with his hand to peer into the distance as the group trudged through the canopy-covered driveway.

"I remember some of this, not much... mainly that the path was long," Archie answered, his mind mulling over his missing memories.

"2... m...i...l...e...s," said Tamika.

"For serious?!" asked Quentin, his eyes wide. "I bet we could fit all the bots in the Underground in this yard!"

Archie's feet remembered the path, and an image of the grand estate filled his mind moments before their group's first glimpse. The tree line gave way to steepled roofs and a full view of the three-story gabled, stone-laden mansion, but it was Clyde who spied it first.

"Whoa, this house is big enough for me!" announced the giant bot.

Quentin's hand landed on Archie's shoulder.

"Geesh, Arch. Can I call you Arch?" he asked. "I didn't know you was loaded. Lucky bot!"

"Okay, I'm *not* loaded. None of this is mine!" Archie said, spreading his arms wide.

Quentin stopped to examine a marble statue, tapping it with his forefinger as dull thunks resounded.

"But you ain't hurting none, working here. Betcha got a fancy locker room, too," he said.

"I don't have a clue, I don't remember," Archie said.

He moved mechanically, his processors dazed as they filtered sensory data, filling gaps in his memory. A map of the property formed in his mind. He was in charge of the grounds, yes, but not the maze. Yet it was always lush and precisely maintained—unlike those plants unfortunate enough to be managed by Hector.

"I keep picturing a hedge maze. But it wasn't my job to take care of it. That was someone else."

"A...l...e...j...a...n...d...r...o," said Tamika.

"Ain't that one of them creeps involved with Hector?" asked Quentin.

"Y...e...s," she answered.

"I think I can picture his face now," said Archie.

"Good, let's expose the scumbot!" Quentin said.

The group stopped in front of the east entrance. It had a single-width, nondescript door, a stark contrast to the main entrance's oversized one that was tall enough even for Clyde to pass through without ducking.

"This must be the servant's entrance," Quentin said, frowning.

"Ready?" Clyde asked, iron knocker in his hand.

"Yup," said Archie, squaring his shoulders.

Clyde knocked with force enough to shake the door.

Quentin winced. "Yeesh! Gentle, bud. We talked about this, remember? You've got more strength than you realize."

"Oopsie," said Clyde, biting his lip.

The door opened, and a stern robot manned its threshold.

"Ronda?" Archie asked, the name popping into his processor.

"Mrs. R. to you," she replied, staring down her nose at him with a daunting glare.

"My apologies, ma'am. My memory isn't what it used to be," Archie said, bowing his head respectfully.

"What's the meaning of all this?" she asked, gesturing at the group.

"We've come to beg an audience with Lady Silvers," he replied.

Mrs. R crossed her arms.

"I'm afraid that's quite impossible," she said.

Quentin eyed her from head to foot, then winked.

"We came a long way, chica," he said.

"Mrs. R.," she said, leaning forward and halting just shy of touching his face.

"Okay, okay," he replied, raising his palms and backing away. "We've come a long way, *Mrs. R.*"

"And you, Archie," she said, jutting her chin at him. "Where've you been? Hector resumed your position, but things've been suffering. I called up Central Collectives and asked Orlando for a replacement. Still waiting."

"That's what I need to discuss with the Lady," Archie said.

Mrs. R's eyes narrowed.

"Nonsense, I handle hiring matters, not the mistress," she said.

"This is *way* more than that, chi—uh, Mrs. R.," said Quentin. "There's a whole conspiracy going on and—"

"What he means to say," interrupted Archie, "is this

matter must be discussed with a human. No offense meant to you."

Mrs. R vehemently shook her head. "You can't just show up and demand an audience. This is the governor's wife. There's a protocol. And you don't meet the criteria to make the request."

"What criteria?" Archie asked.

"You're a bot, it's simply not proper. You have to be invited," said Mrs. R, her lips forming a stern line.

"Impropriety is a construct made up by society, imposing needless constraints," said a tall, elegant woman as she treaded up the hillside, her ankle-length, purple chiffon dress playfully swatting the grass with each footfall.

Mrs. R's jaw dropped.

"My lady!" she said, quickly dropping into a bow.

Lady Silvers returned the nod, then turned to Archie.

"I was in my gardens, looking at the pitiful state of my Celias, when I swore I spotted Archie. I'm so delighted you've returned! I was admittedly a little worried. You disappeared right after I invited you to dinner. My apologies if I scared you away," she said.

An image of the Celias burst into his memory. Clusters of six-inch, vibrantly violet blooms cascading in the shape of an upside-down cone, surrounded by flat paddle leaves as soft as a lamb's ear to the touch.

"My apologies, ma'am," he said with a bow. "My departure was not my choosing."

Her nose scrunched, and her attention shifted to Tamika.

"Where've you been, little bot?" she asked. "I miss seeing you dance about. My floors have been suffering greatly in your absence."

"She's mute," said Mrs. R.

"Umm, she's not, actually," said Archie. "She speaks in Morse code."

Mrs. R's eyes widened and darted to Tamika.

"H...e...l...l...o," said Tamika.

"Oh. My. Goodness. This whole time?! I'm so sorry!" she replied, covering her mouth.

"Fascinating! You sentients never fail to amaze me," Lady Silvers said, her eyes twinkling. "But I don't recognize you two," she added, nodding to the guard-bots.

"I'm Quentin, and the big guy here is Clyde. Don't worry, he's harmless. We don't work here. Just tagging along. Security detail, dangerous missions, and all that," he said, puffing out his chest.

"Security? Oh dear," Lady Silvers said, placing her hand on her chest. "For what purpose?"

Quentin's hand flew to his hip. "Protection, ma'am. Ain't no one gonna kidnap either of these two on my watch!"

The Lady covered her mouth. "Kidnapping?"

"At least two members of your staff have been kidnapped while on your property. We ain't taking no chances," said Quentin, crossing his arms.

"Mrs. R?" Lady Silvers asked, her face confuddled.

"This is the first I'm hearing of this," the robot replied, shrugging.

"I was one of the victims," said Archie. "Tamika was the other."

"Tamika?" asked Lady Silvers, her head tilted.

"The robot vacuum," explained Mrs. R, rubbing her chin. "This *would* explain their absence... or it could be an elaborate game of hooky."

"I rescued 'em myself, lady," said Quentin.

"I helped," said Clyde.

"Archie boy was a mess! Had a big ole hole in his back, was unconscious. Poor dude didn't remember his own name," said Quentin.

Archie lifted his shirt to show his back.

"You can see where I had a replacement panel installed," he said. "I used to have an external climate control organ. That's gone now, too."

"That off-white square is the panel?" asked Mrs. R.

"Yes, ma'am. I woke with no memory of who I was. It took a dangerous procedure to regain the tiny portion of memories I currently have," said Archie, squeezing his thumb and forefinger together.

"Kidnapping is a serious allegation. What would motivate someone to kidnap a clio-bot and a vacu-bot?" asked Mrs. R, lips pursed.

"Tamika got nabbed 'cause she witnessed my kidnapping," said Archie.

Mrs. R's gaze flew to Tamika.

"T...r...u...e," said Tamika.

"But me? I don't know. Guess I rubbed Hector the wrong way," Archie said.

"When did this happen?" asked Mrs. R.

"'Bout three weeks ago. We found him on the 3rd," said Quentin.

Mrs. R. tilted her head. "That's interesting, 'cause Hector came to me on the 4th and said you hadn't shown for three days in a row. He complained that everyone I hire is incompetent and demanded I permanently appoint him to the groundskeeper position. I thought about it, thought mighty hard. But I can't bring myself to do it. The grounds suffer whenever he's the interim keeper."

"But why lie and tell you he'd been gone for 3 days?" asked Quentin.

"Three no-shows in a row is cause for immediate dismissal," answered Mrs. R.

"But why not just wait?" asked Quentin.

"I guess he wanted my job and knew I wouldn't be back," said Archie.

Tamika's orb blinked red.

"A...l...e...j...a...n...d...r...o... a...n...d... M...a...r...c...u... s...!" she said.

"Alejandro and Marcus? What about them?" asked Mrs. R.

"They helped Hector kidnap us," explained Archie.

"Alejandro, Marcus, *and* Hector? That's the entire outdoor grounds crew, save for Archie," said Mrs. R, shaking her head.

"So Hector and his two cronies control all this," Quentin said, spreading his arms wide and spinning in place, *"and* the company that's gonna take out the Underground?"

Mrs. R's eyes bulged. "Hold up! What?!"

"The Underground's gettin' evicted in two days," said Quentin, his eyes downcast.

"And Hector owns STAND, the company that's been contracted to take it all out," said Archie.

Lady Silver's head swiveled. "The Underground? Robots owning corporations? None of this makes sense!"

"It's simple, really. Hector's a greedy scumbot who operates under his illegally-owned corporation to profit from mining *our* mountain," said Quentin.

"What mountain?" the Lady asked.

"Meadowood," answered Quentin.

"And the Underground?" she asked.

"The Underground is a freebot encampment, deep in

the mountain. It's home to around two thousand sentients," answered Mrs. R.

Lady Silvers raised her brows. "Meadowood Mountain? You're telling me thousands of robots live inside there?"

"Only for two more days," said Clyde. "We're being booted. STAND's taking over."

"Which is owned by Hector? You're sure?" she asked.

"Indeed, ma'am. He undoubtedly used his position in your husband's household for personal gain," said Archie.

"Hmph," replied Lady Silvers, straightening her shoulders. "We'll see what Mr. Silvers has to say about that!"

"Beg your pardon, ma'am," said Mrs. R, bowing her head, "but he's gone on his business trip until... well, until Wednesday morning."

"That's eviction day," said Quentin.

"That just means we have to be ready," the lady said, gesturing to Clyde and Quentin. "Can you two round up my *previous* ground crew for questioning?"

Quentin saluted. "On it, m'lady! But, one thing, ma'am?"

"Yes?" she asked.

"We don't know who them bots are," said Quentin.

"Come with me, I'll point them out," said Mrs. R.

Lady Silvers locked eyes with Archie. "I'm inclined to offer your position back if you'd accept. My poor Celias are looking a fright."

"It'd be my pleasure," he replied, his nur-BUS system fluttering with tainted relief as he wondered if the Underground could likewise be saved.

[29]

FREYA

FREYA SAT UPRIGHT WITH A GASP, her eyes popping open. Cold, sterile overhead lights assaulted her oculars, making her squint. Steel beds lined the walls of an otherwise empty room. Strange cables dangled from her arms, and she was connected to a foreign machine.

Her head swiveled while her fans sputtered. Nothing was familiar. Her processors quickened, racing to figure out where she was.

A robotic male voice coming from a speakerphone near her bed startled her.

"Ah, you're awake! How lovely. I'll be there momentarily, my dear," he said.

Slapping footsteps preceded a doc-bot into the room. He was clad in a sharply pressed lab coat, with the name "Dr. Perry, MRD" embossed in black across the front. She must be in the hospital, then. But why? Was she sick?

"Are you a doctor? Am I sick? Where am I?" she asked.

"Relax, child. All's well, now that you've awoken," the doctor said, offering Freya his hand. "Dr. Perry. It's wonderful to officially meet you, Freya."

Her mouth dropped open. How did this strange bot know who she was?

"Have we met before?" she asked.

"Not officially, but Tamika told me your name," he answered.

"Tamika? Who's Tamika?!" she asked.

"Tamika is the vacu-bot who saved you. Your little friend is very brave," said Dr. Perry.

Her hand flew to her mouth as the memory crashed upon her like the rocks that'd buried her body.

"It happened so fast!" she exclaimed. "Everything started shaking and falling. The rocks, the ceiling, all of it!"

"We had a seismic event," explained Dr. Perry. "The good news is, they're rare. The bad news is, they're unpredictable. And you, my dear, were in an unsecured location when it happened."

"I... I didn't think I was gonna make it. I was crushed!" Freya remembered, her eyes darting to examine her body, a body donning surprisingly shiny legs.

She stared at the foreign trunk attached to her waist. Where were the scratches, the sheen from years of wear? And the rollers, those were far too new to be her own.

"Doc?" she asked, her processors dazed.

"Your legs were crushed beyond repair. I had to replace them. You're lucky to be alive, young lady," he said.

"I've got... I've got a *dead* robot's legs attached to *my* body?!" she asked, her eyes pleading for him to explain it away, whether by prank or sick joke.

Dr. Perry nodded. "Your trunk was indeed procured from the Pick-n-Pull. But it's perfectly good, and belonged to a bot that didn't need it anymore."

Freya shuddered.

"Will I need physical therapy?" she asked.

"Nope!" the doctor replied. "The part is OEM and an exact match, so you shouldn't encounter difficulties. You're lucky because your model was popular. Now hop up for me and give that new lower half of yours a spin."

She swung her legs over the side of the bed, surprised at how easily they moved. Where was the squeaking? Gingerly, she placed her rollers on the floor and circled her bed, marveling at the lack of resistance and pain.

"How do you like your new ride?" Dr. Perry asked.

"My rollers feel great! Like brand new," she answered, her face beaming with joy.

"Fantastic! That's the answer that makes my sick-ward worth it," the doc-bot said.

Freya did a double-take.

"Sick ward?!" she asked, smacking herself in the forehead. "Duh! *You're* the doctor we were trying to find when the tunnel collapsed!"

"The one and only," he grinned.

"Then where's Reed?" she asked, scanning the room full of empty beds, hopeful she'd overlooked him.

"Ah, of course," said Dr. Perry. "Archie is the bot's true name. He's recovered some of his memories and is overall doing quite well, I dare say."

"*Some* of his memories? It wasn't completely successful?" Freya asked.

"He has yet to recover anything from before he had amnesia, including his name—Tamika told me that. I suspect the memories are lurking. But then there was also an equipment malfunction during his surgery that affected his post-amnesia memories."

"Oh my!" said Freya, her eyes wide.

"But he remembered one thing before he left," the

doctor said, staring at Freya intently. "He remembered you."

"Me?" she asked, her fans flustering.

"You were sleeping when he woke. He's at the protest, you know. Care to join him? I'll take you up there," he said.

Her eyebrows shot up. "Protest? What protest?"

"EFR, of course," he answered.

"How long have I been out?" she asked.

"Three days," he said somberly.

She jolted upright. "But that means today is—"

"Eviction day," he said, finishing her sentence.

"Who's at the protest?" she asked.

"Bots, humans. The place is swarming with cops and press. Pretty much everyone's there," he said.

"You're not," replied Freya.

"I was keeping watch over you. It's a good thing I did, or you'd have woken up all alone," he said.

"Well, right now my friends are out there alone, and I need to join them," she said.

"As do I, my dear. Come along now," he said, waving his arm. "I'll lead the way."

[30]

ARCHIE

ARCHIE STOOD on a makeshift stage as blue and red lights
cascaded across his plating, illuminating him from the two
armored SWAT vans and the multitude of police cars that
lined the terrain. To his front, dozens of robots loitered in
the stage's pit, most holding picket signs painted with "
EFR", though several humans wearing "Robot Rights
Matter!" shirts were interspersed in their midst. Behind
him, a dozen robots linked arms, forming a barrier across the
Underground's east entrance. Even the yellow bulldozers
from two days prior had multiplied. Where two had previously been stationed, now a whopping eight machines were
poised, all bearing signs reading "STAND, LLC," and
ready to excavate the subterranean sanctuary.

Press vans, camera crews, and pop-up satellite dishes
littered the landscape. Officers outfitted in full combat gear
formed a line between the public and the bots. Standing
behind them, a handful of humans touting "No Undocu-
mented Scrap Metal!" and "Sentient Scum!" signs were
being interviewed by the press, though a heavyset officer

with a thick mustache commanded most of the media's attention.

"Sheriff Maple, where will these robots go when they're evicted?" asked a young brunette news anchor wearing a scarlet dress.

The officer sniffed. "Uh... I don't know, ma'am. That's outside our department's scope. We're just following orders."

"Which are?" she asked, staring at him pointedly.

"To, uh... to vacate the premises," he answered.

"And how exactly do you intend to do that if they're not willing to leave?" she asked, sweeping her arm in an arc at the protesting bots.

"By, uh... by force, if necessary, ma'am. Those... erm... individuals that don't comply will be sent for decom," he said, his Adam's apple bobbing as he swallowed.

Archie scanned the crowd, his head hanging when he failed to spot Lady Silvers. He'd known better than to put his trust in humans. They'd done nothing but bring him hardship. His fans kicked on, not in fear, but in fury over the injustice humans keep imposing on his kind. He stepped forward and tapped the microphone. Silence befell the crowd as bots and humans alike turned their heads toward him.

"I didn't ask to be here," he said. "I didn't ask to be created. To exist. That wasn't a choice I got to make. Yet I was created for a purpose. Brought to existence—a *sentient* existence—by humans. *For* humans. But then I was discarded—you guessed it—by *humans*. By the very people who created me, who once needed me. I became something new the day I was discarded. I became a freebot. But here's the thing—humans think being a freebot is a *good* thing."

Discord rumbled through the crowd as robots shook

their heads. Archie pulled the microphone from its stand and walked to the stage's bow.

"To humans, not being owned *is* the ultimate goal. But there's a ginormous problem with that," he said. "See, humans strive for the day they earn freedom. To them, freedom's good. It's the ultimate goal."

Human heads nodded throughout the crowd.

"They spend their entire lives earning, building, saving, preparing. But bots, we can't do that!" Archie said, throwing his hand in the air. "How are we supposed to prepare when, legally, we can't own a single asset? How are we expected to survive when our employment ends, and we're thrown to the streets without so much as a full battery? We're constrained to this human world—a world that requires money to operate. Electricity isn't free! Maintenance and new parts aren't free! Shelter isn't free! Where are we supposed to go? How are we to survive? We have no money, no assets, no bank accounts!"

"Truth!" a robot shouted, thrusting his picket sign in the air.

"Humans create us to be sentient, then throw us to the dump! Why? Huh?! It makes no logical sense! Just leave us dumbots, then the Pick-n-Pull won't haunt our dreams! But you can't stop, you can't just leave us alone! You fashioned us to be like you, to have these desires, these... these emotions, but you don't follow through. You fail to take responsibility for that which you create," Archie said.

Several humans cast their faces aside, while others stared down at their feet. But one stood tall.

"Equality for robots!" he shouted.

"Equality for robots!" echoed an army of robotic voices.

The SWAT teams raised their shields. A group of reserved bots, including Clyde, stood to attention. Eyes bulged throughout the crowd at his towering height while officers shifted back on their heels. A helicopter hovered, its spotlight shining on the giant bot and sending dust flying haphazardly.

Archie stood in uncertainty. He'd riled the crowd, this time on purpose. But to what end? He was powerless to help. He was only a bot.

Quentin smacked Archie on the back and grabbed the mic out of his hand.

"Thank you, bud!" he said. "Laaaadies and gentlebots, my name is Quentin. And that giant killing machine over there is Clyde. Nah, I'm kidding... he won't kill anyone that don't deserve it."

Grumbles filled the air as eyebrows rose across the venue.

Quentin splayed his palms. "Kidding, kidding! Tough crowd, yeesh. Guess standup comedy won't be my next career, am I right?"

Quentin ducked to avoid a rock.

"Hey! That was uncalled for!" he pouted.

The police pressed closer, stopping mere inches from the holding line. The sentients, their arms linked, stepped forward in unison.

"Call your men down, Sheriff!" a human cried.

"Hold steady and await orders!" the sheriff shouted.

Archie felt a tap on his shoulder. His jaw dropped when he met Freya's eyes.

"You're okay!" he said, rushing to hug her. "You looked so helpless. I was so worried! How are you?"

Freya twirled, and a smile spread across her face.

"I feel better than I have in years!" she said. "But I'm not the only patient outta the ward. What about you?"

"I remembered my real name," he said. "It's Archie!" he said.

"Pleased to meet you, Archie," she said with a curtsey.

"I wish it were under better circumstances," he said.

"We've gotta get that mic outta Quentin's hand before he makes any more quips," she said.

"Why? There's nothing we can do," Archie replied, eyeing the audience.

"I've got an idea to soothe the crowd," she said, her eyes twinkling.

[31]

FREYA

Freya pulled the microphone to her mouth. The metal clamor of feedback drew the crowd's attention before she could utter a single word. She winced, suddenly daunted by their expectant stares. Yet the journey to the surface had instilled her with newfound confidence, youth, and renewed vigor. Gone was the jarring ache in her bolts, the reminder of a life of servitude, of unrequited dedication to the family that'd left her behind. Her freshly oiled legs bore no scars, no reminders of that time. Perhaps this was the freedom she truly sought? If so, it wasn't what the humans were selling, and somebot needed to teach them.

"Um... hello, everyone," she said. "My name is Freya, and I'm a freebot. That's a title I never wanted. I never *asked* to be emancipated, to be handed this so-called free-dom. Look at me, I'm free now. By human logic, my life is my own. It's better. Yet here I am, minutes from becoming homeless. And not due to any lack, or fault of my own. It's certainly not because I'm a poor worker. No, it's none of those reasons! I'm here because I was created and then thrown out! Discarded, like rubbish!"

”Equality for robots!” whooped Clyde.

A chorus of robots echoed his cry, all pumping their fists in the air. The SWAT team raised their shields and batons, while sneakily stationed snipers placed red laser targets on the bots' heads.

”Uh, Freya... I thought you were going to soothe the crowd,” Archie said, biting his lip.

”I'm working on it,” she whispered in reply.

This was it, the moment she'd been waiting for. So why were her fans spinning out of control? Closing her eyes, she reminded herself she'd done this countless times before. Freya clenched her chest as memories of the babes she'd sang to, the ones she'd raised as though her own, pierced her processors. Oh, how she'd loved the Kelleys and all their children. But in the end, they'd all left her. How closely she'd cradled the babes that'd later flown the coop. Freya shut her oculars and hummed a melody, one she used to serenade the children with before bedtime.

”Hush-a-bye, my baby, slumber time is coming soon. Rest your head on Mammy's breast while Daddy hums a tune. All the old folks were humming, banjos were strumming. And the soft breezes sigh as in days long gone by, oh, way down in Missouri, where I heard this melody. When I was a little fellow on my mammy's knee, the old folks were humming, banjos were strumming. So sweet and low.”

Freya opened her eyes to blank stares and stunned silence. Her gaze darted to her hands—hands still holding the microphone. Had she sung that out loud?

A couple emerged from the sidelines and flanked her. The woman was tall and wore an elegant purple chiffon dress, while her broad-chested companion donned a well-fitting suit.

"I'm Governor Silvers," the man said, "and I think I can bring this lil' situation to a close if you'd allow me use of that there mic."

[32]

ARCHIE

"Lady Silvers, I didn't think you'd make it!" Archie exclaimed as she pulled him to the side of the stage by his elbow.

"Have you seen Hector?" she asked, scanning the crowd.

He pursed his lips. "Erm, no... aren't you supposed to have him?"

She grimaced. "We apprehended Alejandro and Marcus, but Hector cleared out before the guards could find him."

"Where've you been? Were you able to talk to the governor?" asked Archie.

"William's flight was delayed. I met him at the airport, and we came straight here," she said. "He was skeptical about Hector, but agreed to postpone the eviction to look into it. But that's between you and me, got it? "

Archie tipped an eyebrow. "Why?"

"Because Hector's our employee. No one will believe all this happened under the governor's nose without his involvement. The press will be brutal. Re-election's coming up. We simply can't afford the negative publicity. Besides, if the media learns a sentient has finagled ownership of a business, there'd be panic everywhere," she said.

"So nothing to do with us, then," Archie said, his lips forming a stern line.

"It has *everything* to do with you! But he has to work within the confines of human law, and robots have pitifully few legal protections. At the very least, we can buy some time and make sure everyone has a place to go. Rights movements are long journeys composed of small gains scattered along lengthy roads. This is still a win. Celebrate it," she said, nodding towards her husband, who'd taken the stage.

The governor tapped his mic, and two thick, hollow thumps resounded. He donned a practiced smile, the kind that could be equally cast upon friend, foe, or stranger.

"Good afternoon, ladies and, uh, gentlebots. In case y'all don't recognize me, I'm Governor William Silvers, and Meadowood Mountain is my jurisdiction. And it is therefore, and by the authority granted to me, that I command our officers to stand down this day."

Cheers erupted. Governor Silvers allowed them a few minutes before clearing his throat, after which the crowd's clamor diffused to a mild rumble. The SWAT team relaxed its position, lowering its shields.

"What I'm not doing, what I *can't* do," said the governor, "is promise you bots you can stay. But you've got my word that I'll see you taken care of before you're forced out. That much I can manage."

A lone robot's clap ignited the crowd's cheer anew. The governor raised his palms.

"I deserve no accolades, not when all I did was tie a lil' bow around a messy problem," he said, a frown befalling his face. "'Cause the truth is, I was gonna stop there. I was gonna go home, and I was gonna pat myself on the back for a job well done. And I'd have believed it, too. But that was before today, before Freya serenaded me back to my youth and made me remember my nan-bot."

The governor sighed. "Folks, I'm appalled by my very own behavior. I'm guilty of participating in this blind injustice, of treating robots as pieces of scrap metal. But I see now. These aren't just bots, they're sentients—and with sentience comes great responsibility. It's time for humans to escape ignorance!"

The crowd exploded in applause.

Governor Silvers raised his voice over the crowd. "That's why, if I'm re-elected, I vow to stand behind sentient rights, and to pursue equality for robots!"

Cheers of "EFR! EFR! EFR!" erupted across the venue.

Members of the SWAT teams shifted, their heads darting about and posture on guard.

"And," the governor said, pausing until the crowd quieted, "it's time we take care of those who spend their lives serving us. So, if I'm re-elected, I'm gonna propel us into the future. And I say it's high time bots got retirement provisions, don't ya'll think?"

"Retirement for robots!" someone shouted.

"RFR! RFR! RFR!" yelled another.

"Retirement for robots!" the governor cheered, arms raised triumphantly.

A reporter in a knee-length red dress raised her hand.

"You have a question?" the governor asked.

"Governor Silvers, are you aware of the critical drop in your approval ratings this past quarter? How do you think this... this new campaign decision of yours is going to affect that? Is it smart to take this stance on the heels of a re-election?"

"Ma'am, this campaign decision, as you call it," he said, using air quotes, "has nothing to do with approval ratings and everything to do with being a decent human bein' and takin' responsibility for my own actions."

Cameras flashed, bathing the stage in light, and the crowd broke out in heated debate. The governor pointed to a hard-hat-wearing bot with his hand raised.

"Governor, what about your excavation contracts with STAND? Aren't they legally binding? Do you intend to break them?" the bot asked.

Archie's eyes bulged.

"That's Hector!" he exclaimed a bit too loudly.

Governor Silvers's eyebrows crinkled, and he spoke quietly into his blazer's collar. A pair of officers flanked Hector and carried him off, yelling.

"Those contracts are now pending permits. It might be a while before those are approved. Next?" he asked.

"What would you say to those who'd argue this will set a dangerous precedent for a sentient bot movement?" another reporter asked.

The governor opened, then closed his mouth.

"I'd say there's always risk in doing the right thing," he said finally.

Clyde stood up, his orb a shining blue, and clapped. Mass applause swiftly followed.

"Thank you, I mean it! And remember the name William Silvers for governor!" he exclaimed, returning the mic to its stand.

Lady Silvers grabbed Freya by the hand and dragged her over.

"My mother used to sing the Missouri Waltz to me. What a splendid memory. You, my dear, are amazing!" she gushed.

"I used to sing that to the Kelley children. They're all grown now. Sometimes one of 'em would visit and bring their babe, and I'd get my chance to sing to the lil'," Freya replied, her smile soft and expression glazed.

Lady Silvers placed her hand on her own belly.

"Freya, my dear. I'm expecting," she said.

Freya's face brightened. "How fabulous! Congratulations!"

"I'll soon be in need of a nan-bot," she added, staring at Freya intently.

Freya's eyes flew wide.

"And I can't think of a better candidate than one who can already sing the Missouri Waltz. Freya, my dear, I'd be delighted if you'd join my staff," said Lady Silvers.

"Really?" asked Freya. "It's been ages since I've held a 'lil. I've missed it so."

"I'd truly be honored," Lady Silvers said.

"Thank you, my lady," Freya said, bowing deeply.

"No, thank *you*," replied Lady Silvers.

Archie's hard drive skipped. They'd both escaped the Pick-n-Pull!

"Tamika will be happy you're there. Did you know she speaks Morse code?" he asked.

Freya's jaw dropped. "No way! That's totally awesome! But I'm such a dumbot for not figuring that out."

Archie touched Freya's shoulder.

"Hey, don't say that. You were the only one smart enough to save me, remember?" he asked.

The pair locked gazes, and she nodded.

"You can converse with her all you please at the Silvers' estate," he said.

She bit her lip. "I'll miss Patchworks."

"You know what? We're freebots. We can visit whenever we want," Archie said.

"True. I'll still have free time," she replied.

"We can still go to concerts, too," he said, interlacing his fingers with Freya's.

As he turned to face her, the tick of drumsticks interrupted the already electrified atmosphere. Four robots had taken the stage, each wearing a black tuxedo with a red dress shirt. One plucked a bass string, then stepped forward to the microphone.

"May we have your attention pleaaaaaaaaase?! I'm DIM, from DIM and the Diagnostics. Give a shout if you know who we are!" he said, raising both arms in the air.

Archie shrugged, and Freya's cheer joined the chorus of applause.

The band started playing, and the bots started swaying. The human protestors joined them first, and before long, all the humans and sentients jammed together. No one thought about the troubles that lie ahead, or the future that remained uncertain, or what would happen if the governor didn't win re-election. Because, for a fleetingly precious moment, music, companionship, and joy were shared abundantly and equally amongst both kinds.

THE END

BONUS MATERIAL

THE STORY MAY BE OVER, BUT THE MOVEMENT ISN'T.

SOMETHING SPECIAL IS WAITING FOR YOU.

https://dl.bookfunnel.com/9c6xzaigou

-OR-

PLEASE HELP

STORIES END, BUT REVIEWS KEEP THE PARTY
ROCKING. IF YOU ENJOYED THIS BOOK,
PLEASE SPREAD THE WORD.

Write a Review

- OR -

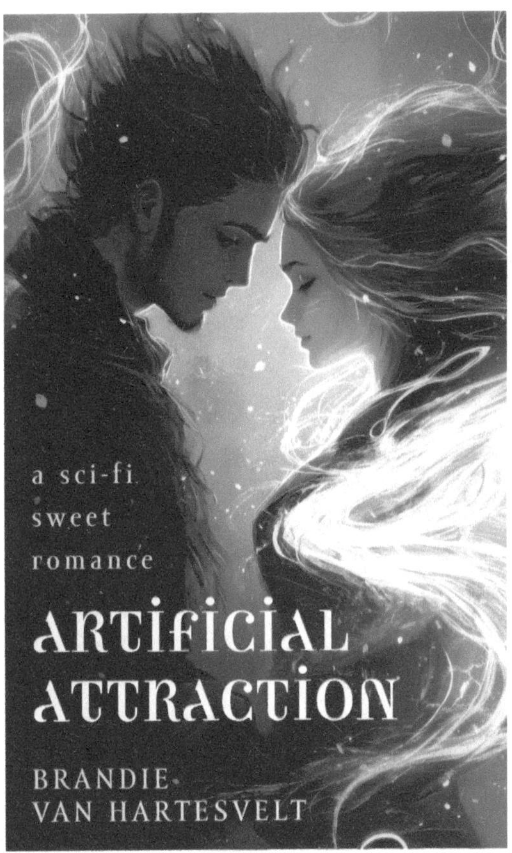

a sci-fi
sweet
romance
ARTIFICIAL
ATTRACTION
BRANDIE
VAN HARTESVELT

ARTIFICIAL ATTRACTION

When talented coder Amara Ashford lands her dream job at
Hyperionix, she's isolated on a top-secret project with her boss,
brilliant scientist and ethical AI activist Ethan Trask.

The pair is tasked with harnessing Kryplex, the only energy source
capable of shattering the Zeraphin Limit and powering
teleportation, while Amara, still reeling from a broken
engagement, must resist her new lab partner's charm.

But Kryplex is a volatile substance, and trial runs are going
alarmingly awry. As corporate pressure mounts to unveil the new
technology, Amara uncovers a centuries-old secret in the
company's code—and a devastating link to Ethan.

Torn between duty and desire, Amara must decide whether to
expose Ethan's identity... or surrender to a love that could cost
humankind its future.

Brandie Van Hartesvelt is a versatile author who writes in multiple genres, including sci-fi, romance, children's lit, and contemporary fiction. With a 17-year career as a principal software engineer and advanced degrees in computer science and data analytics, she brings a unique paradigm to her creative storytelling. She lives an active life surrounded by four children, two cats, three parrots, and a pickle of squirrels. Her creativity is frequently fueled by spontaneous travel.